JOY

Duckula's Holiday Camp Adventure

CARNIVAL

Carnival
An imprint of the Children's Division
of the Collins Publishing Group
8 Grafton Street, London W1X 3LA

Published by Carnival 1989

Count Duckula is a registered trademark of
THAMES TELEVISION plc.
Copyright © Cosgrove Hall Productions 1989

ISBN 0 00 194877 6

Printed and bound in Great Britain by
Collins, Glasgow

Set in Times

1

Duckula's Bright Idea!

It was a hot, sultry night in the Transylvanian Alps. *What*, you say? No crashing thunder? No lightning streaking across the dark sky, illuminating the jagged outline of Castle Duckula in a terrifying manner? No cringing peasants, scurrying for cover from the teeming rain?

Give us a break, reader! It's got to be nice *sometime* in Transylvania!

Anyway, it was hot and sticky and horrible – and Count Duckula was tucked up tightly in bed and trying to get to sleep.

'Boy!' he sighed, flinging back the bedclothes. 'There's a heatwave in Transylvania and Nanny has to give me woolly sheets, woolly blankets – and these itchy woolly pyjamas!'

The bedroom door burst open with a loud splintering noise; not on its hinges, like most doors, but vertically downwards like a drawbridge!

'Hey! What the – ?' Duckula sat upright in fright.

It was Nanny: sixteen stones (that's 102 kilos for smart-alec readers!) of good-natured flesh and chicken bones. She was carrying a small record-player.

'Only me, Duckyboos!' she squawked.

'Yes, I gathered that,' replied Duckula drily. 'The smashed-down door that comes before you is always a dead give-away!'

'The door's given way?' Nanny blinked. 'Oh, yes. Funny 'ow they always do in this place!'

'What do you want?' demanded Duckula.

'I 'eard you tossin' an' turnin' in bed,' began Nanny. 'So I thought I'd bring you a little treat.'

'Great!' Duckula was pleased. What had she brought him? A radio-controlled car? A cricket bat? A home computer?

Nanny placed the record-player on the bedside table and opened up the lid. Then she turned to face Duckula and produced from her sling a small pile of records. 'It's me Frankie Fledgling record collection!' she beamed. 'Lovely relaxin' songs to send you to sleep!'

Duckula groaned. 'They'll do that all right, Nanny – but what a way to go! I think I'd prefer a cyanide pill!'

'Oooh, I *loves* a good tune!' Nanny purred blissfully as she wound up the clockwork motor of the record-player.

'So do I – and that's why I don't want to hear any of your records,' complained Duckula, covering up his ears.

Nanny was too engrossed in choosing a record to listen to Duckula's protests. At length she selected a well-worn disc from its sleeve and laid it on the turntable. 'This is me favourite, Duckyboos – "Sunshine, Strawberries An' 'You".'

A dreadful orchestra struck up a dreadful tune, followed by some dreadful words sung by a cheerful-sounding man who couldn't sing. Nanny hopped from one foot to the other and twirled round and round, waving her arm and sling in the air.

'For Pete's sake, Nanny!' yelled Duckula, wrapping a sheet round his head. 'Turn it off!'

Far below this tuneless extravaganza, in the damp, dark depths of the Castle's dungeons, Igor the butler was busily oiling the chains and manacles that hung from the rough stone walls. He hummed a dreary funeral march in his deep voice as he fondled the chains lovingly. You simply have to keep the torture chamber in tip-top order, he mused; after all, you never know who might drop in.

The awful strains of Frankie's voice floated down through the Castle and interrupted Igor's humming. He stood back, aghast, dropped his oilcan and covered his ears with his hands.

'I can take a lot,' he murmured, shaking his head sadly. 'I can take the low salary . . . the long hours . . . the humiliation of looking after a – a *vegetarian* master, but I cannot take Nanny's choice in music!'

'Funny,' squawked Nanny loudly over the music. 'Frankie always sounds better on the wireless than 'e does on me record-player!'

'No wonder!' yelled back Duckula. 'You're ruining your records playing them on that ancient relic of a gramophone!'

Nanny blinked and pulled the arm off the record. '*Phone*, did you say, Duckyboos?' She cocked her head to one side and listened intently. 'I can't hear no phone ringin'!'

'I said *gram-o-phone* – not telephone!'

'What? Oh, gramophone! Yes, I knew you'd like it

7

– I'll play you some more!' With that, she replaced the arm on the offending record and the terrible din resumed.

Suddenly into the bedroom strode Igor, wearing his overcoat. In one hand he carried a hurriedly packed suitcase, and in the other a letter in an envelope. He marched across to Duckula's bed and placed the envelope on his master's knees.

'Say, what's this, Igor? It's a little late for the post, isn't it?'

'It's my resignation, milord,' Igor said shortly. He turned and made for the door.

'Igor, come back!' cried Duckula, grappling with his heavy woollen blankets and scrambling out of bed. 'What's the matter?!'

'Do I really need to spell it out, sir?' barked Igor in a huff, staring at Nanny, who was still weaving and jumping and rotating to Frankie Fledgling.

'Say no more, Igor.' Duckula raised his voice to screaming pitch and screamed at the top of his voice. 'KNOCK IT OFF, NANNY – PLEASE!!!'

Nanny stopped almost in mid air. Then, with a puzzled expression, she gave her record-player a deliberate jab with her elbow, sending it crashing to the floor. It smashed with a horrible twanging sound.

'There, I've knocked it off, Duckyboos – but I can't think why on earth you asked me to do it,' she said sulkily. 'It's broken now!'

'Give me strength!' sighed Duckula. 'I didn't mean knock it off! I just meant – oh, never mind. It solves one problem anyway. I presume you're staying now, Igor?'

'Well,' replied the butler in a grumpy voice, 'if I may have your assurance, milord that it won't happen again – '

'It can't happen again!' confirmed Duckula, surveying the heap of broken wood and little cogwheels on the floor.

'And if you can assure me that my time is my own between midnight and dawn – '

'Yes, Igor, yes,' nodded Duckula irritably.

'And if you agree, as we've discussed before, to my having three full weekends off each century – '

'Yes, yes, yes, of course! Honestly, Igor, you've been so grumpy lately, I think it's high time you had a holiday.'

'Well, in that case, I'll reconsider my resignation, milord.'

''Ere, why 'ave you got your coat on, Mr Igor?' screeched Nanny. 'Are you goin' somewhere?'

Duckula tutted. 'Take the rest of the evening off, Igor,' he said.

'Thank you, sir.' Igor stepped over the broken door and disappeared from the bedroom.

'Ooh, 'e gets on me nerves, Duckyboos,' confided Nanny. 'Sometimes I thinks there's somethin' wrong with 'im!'

'You've only just noticed, Nanny?' joked Duckula – but Nanny failed to smile. 'Never mind, let me help you pack up the remains of Frankie Fledgling.'

The young Count bent down and passed the records to Nanny. A colourful little magazine caught his eye. He picked it out and studied the front cover, which had a picture of Frankie sitting on the bonnet of a big

American car, surrounded by a dozen or so adoring fans.

'What's this, Nanny?'

'Oooh, I've been lookin' for that for ages!' beamed Nanny. 'It's Frankie's fan club magazine. You can read it if you want!'

Duckula flicked through the pages. Each one was packed with pictures of the singer: in some he was on-stage in front of crowds of spectators; in others he could be seen talking and laughing to well-known film stars; and in one he was actually shaking hands with the President of the United States of America!

'He seems to have a good time, this Frankie,' said Duckula, intrigued by the pictures. 'He's not stuck in a mouldy old castle all day with nothing to do. Why, I've never even met the Mayor of Transylvania!'

'Oh, yes, 'e goes all over the world!' enthused Nanny. 'An' look, 'ere's Frankie's Favourites page. 'Is favourite food is cheese vegeburgers, an' 'is favour-ite cars are 'is vintage Rolls-Royce an' is gold-plated Cadillac – '

'Vegeburgers? Rolls-Royces? Cadillacs? Let me see!' demanded Duckula, snatching the magazine from Nanny and examining it. 'Favourite pastime – cruising in his luxury yacht; favourite holiday haunt – the Bahamas! Say, this is the life, Nanny – and he can't even *sing* properly! He's not specially good-looking either . . . his beak's too long!'

'Don't you be so wicked!' shrilled Nanny, retrieving her magazine and inserting it into her sling for safety.

'Fame and fortune – that's the key to happiness!'

exclaimed Duckula. 'Nanny, *I'm* going to be a famous singer!'

'*You*, Duckyboos?!' squawked Nanny. 'That would never do! Who'd be master of the castle? Who would I have to look after?'

'Think big, Nanny – oh, I'm sorry, you already do!' laughed the count. 'There's not a second to lose. The moment has arrived for me to enter the big time. Now, where do I begin? How did Frankie Fledgling launch his career?'

'Oh, that's easy!' babbled Nanny, keen to discuss her heart-throb. ''E was an entertainer in an 'oliday camp – an' an important man from the television spotted 'im!' She produced her magazine again and pointed to an old black-and-white photograph of a young Frankie dressed in a funny bathing costume, posing on a poolside diving board.

Duckula looked at it and then waved the magazine in the air. 'An entertainer in a holiday camp, eh? I see, I see! Just one thing, Nanny – what exactly *is* a holiday camp?'

'Ooh, silly! 'Oliday camps is lovely places! Lots of little chalets to stay in . . . with a swimmin' pool . . . an' all sorts of other amusements like dancin' an' bingo. An' they 'ave special people called Yellow-beaks – like what Frankie was – to make it all jolly for you!'

Duckula was enthralled. He stared into space, deep in thought.

'You all right, Duckyboos?' asked Nanny, concerned.

11

He turned to her with bright eyes and spoke in a voice trembling with excitement. 'Nanny,' he said slowly, 'tomorrow we're off to one of these holiday camps!'

2
Making Plans

It was an unusual breakfast time for Duckula the following morning. Instead of gobbling up his normal triple-sized helping of broccoli sandwiches, he merely nibbled absent-mindedly at one sandwich whilst he studied a sheaf of colourful papers that lay in front of him.

'Oooh, you've 'ardly touched your breakfast, Duckyboos!' moaned Nanny, placing a steaming mug of cocoa in front of him. 'I don't know – I wish I 'adn't found them ol' Duckling's 'Oliday Camp brochures for you!'

Duckula didn't even look up. He simply turned over the page of one of the brochures and read it eagerly.

'Can you 'ear me, me young feller?' demanded Nanny. 'Nanny's talkin' to you! Drink your cocoa while it's 'ot. It's got lovely chocolatey bits floatin' on top – jus' the way you likes it.' She shook her head and busied herself by cleaning the stove.

Duckula, still concentrating on his brochures, stretched out a hand and felt around the table for his cocoa. His hand closed round a small vase of Transylvanian daisies that Nanny had picked freshly that morning. He drew the vase towards him and then, still without looking, put the vase to his lips and drank the water.

'Yuck!' The taste of water and petals brought him to his senses. He looked at the vase and spat out. 'Nanny, come and help me. I can't decide!'

'Can't decide what, Duckyboos? Oooh, there's no need to drink the *flowers*! What's wrong with your cocoa?'

Duckula ignored her silly question. 'I can't decide which holiday camp to go to,' he said.

'They're all in Britain.'

'I know that – but Britain's a big place. They've got camps everywhere – Chigwell, Chorlton-cum-Hardy, Glasgow, Shepton Mallet, Pimlico, Salford, Stoke Poges, Wolverhampton – '

'They *all* sound very nice,' declared Nanny.

'Ah, here's one – Bacteria-on-Sea. At least it's at the seaside.'

'You can't beat the seaside, that's what I always say,' cooed Nanny. Then she stopped wiping the stove. ''Ere, did you say *Bacteria-on-Sea*?'

'Yes. Why?'

'I do believe that's the very place Frankie Fledgling started singin'!'

'Really?' exclaimed Duckula. 'Boy, that must be a good omen! Right, Bacteria-on-Sea it is!'

The weather had changed dramatically overnight and now heavy rain was beating at the kitchen windows. A flash of lightning forked across the dark sky and thunder rumbled as Igor walked into the kitchen. He looked considerably brighter than the night before and Duckula thought for a second that he detected a sparkle in his sad, drooping eyes.

14

'Morning, Igor! Miserable weather cheered you up?' he asked cheekily.

'*Ra – ther*, sir!' replied Igor, rubbing his hands together. 'It looks as if the storm's set in for the day. Can't see a break in the clouds anywhere!'

'What a pity you won't be here to enjoy it!' grinned Duckula. 'I'm hoping for lots of sunshine in Bacteria-on-Sea!'

'*What-on-where*, milord? Sounds like a disease.'

'Bacteria-on-Sea, England, Igor. That's where we're going after breakfast. I told you last night that you needed a holiday – and this morning you're on the way. Can't beat that for service, can you?'

'Oh, dear,' murmured Igor darkly. 'And I thought it was going to be a *good* day.'

'That's precisely what it *is* going to be!' cackled Duckula. 'The best day of my life!'

'Hmm, sir, I seem to have heard that before – on a number of occasions.'

'You're right, Mr Igor,' added Nanny. 'There was the time when 'e decided to go explorin' in Darkest Africa . . . an' when 'e wanted to become a champion racin' driver . . . an' when 'e went flyin' in that airship – '

'Until he ran out of gas!' chuckled Igor uncontrollably. 'Oh, dear me! Ha, ha, ha, ha!'

'Okay, okay, you two!' cried Duckula indignantly. 'I didn't ask for a wisecracking routine from the world's worst comedy duo!'

A little door opened quickly in the castle clock and Sviatoslav the bat shot out. 'Dmitri! Dmitri!' he called.

15

'What is it, Sviatoslav?' asked his friend.

'Did you hear that? The duck called his butler and nanny the world's worst comedy duo . . .'

'Huh! The cheek of it!' replied Dmitri. 'They'll have to fight *us* for the title first!'

The two bats screamed with laughter and wobbled back into the clock.

'Milord, I really must protest at your decision just to take the Castle off to England at a moment's notice,' mumbled Igor, stumbling down the dungeon steps behind Duckula and Nanny. 'I'm just not ready to go waltzing off like this. I have things to do.'

'Like what?' grinned Duckula. 'An afternoon prowl round the village? An evening stroll with the werewolf?'

'Very *droll*, sir. But I have the month's supplies to order from the greengrocer . . . and I have the electricity bill to pay . . .'

'I thought we got our electricity from the lightning,' said Duckula.

'I fear you've been reading too many horror stories, sir,' replied Igor with a guilty chuckle.

'Huh, I think not, Igor. There's enough horror in this creepy place to last a lifetime. Anyway, we're going to Bacteria-on-Sea, whether you like it or not. Check your employment contract, I think you'll find *I'm* the boss and *you're* my butler.'

'Do cheer up, Mr Igor!' squawked Nanny brightly. 'We'll have a wonderful time by the sea. It's the journey there that bothers me. I 'ates it when the Castle moves. Last time it nearly shook me beak loose!'

16

Duckula led the little party to the ornate upright coffin, which in reality was the nerve-centre of the Castle's amazing, magical transport system. As he entered it, the coffin hummed into life and the coloured lamps that surrounded it began to flash on and off.

'Just like the end of the pier!' joked Duckula. 'Now, hold on to your hats – *we're off!*'

Igor grasped an iron banister firmly, but Nanny followed Duckula's instructions to the letter and, with her one good arm, simply held on to the little maid's cap on her head. I wonder why 'e told me to do this, she wondered; surely it would make more sense to steady meself by holding onto something more solid. But that's the trouble with Nanny – she never learns!

Duckula slammed the coffin door and did what he had to do in the coffin. Sorry, reader – it's all too secret to let you know the precise details. It's a closely guarded secret known only to the noble Duckula dynasty, passed on from generation to generation by . . . oh, go on then, I'll tell you: he just pressed a couple of knobs here and there and pulled a lever or two and told the Castle where to go!

The Castle began to shake. Igor's knees began to shake. A brilliant glow appeared in the sky around the huge stone monstrosity (that's the Castle – *not* Nanny!) and a loud humming noise filled the air. Peasants ran for cover as loose rocks became dislodged on the mountainside and tumbled down on the village below.

Suddenly, in a rainbow-like aura of vivid, pulsating colours, the Castle vanished with an unearthly whooshing sound.

17

Inside, Nanny lost her balance and rolled like a giant, soft ball to the far end of the dungeon. The Castle tilted sharply as it whizzed invisibly through space – and Nanny came rolling back along the sloping floor at full speed. She collided with Igor, knocking him to the ground like a skittle, and then crashed into the opposite wall. Igor, dazed, held his head and rose unsteadily to his feet. The Castle tilted again – and Nanny was on the move once more. She rolled helplessly back in the other direction, bowling Igor over again.

'*Every time*, Nanny! Every time the Castle moves you insist on throwing yourself around like this!' snapped Igor angrily, remaining on the floor and rubbing his grazed elbows and knees. 'Why can't you keep a hold of yourself?'

Before Nanny was capable of giving an answer, the Castle arrived at its destination and grew still and quiet once more.

'Handbrake on, into neutral,' quipped Duckula. He jumped from the coffin and whistled as he surveyed the bedraggled, tangled mass of Igor and Nanny that lay before him. 'Boy! We have here the most advanced transport system known to man or beast – *mostly beast*, I admit. It can whisk you off to virtually anywhere in the universe in the twinkling of an eye . . . yet you two always look as if you've arrived on the back of a dustcart.'

'Well, I 'eld on to me '*at*,' said Nanny proudly. 'Look – it's still on me 'ead!'

'What *are* you talking about?' asked Duckula, mystified. 'Oh, never mind. We're in Bacteria-on-Sea – at least I *hope* we are! Let's go and see what it's like!'

The young Count bounded up the steps and urged his two servants to walk faster: 'Come on! Aren't you both excited?'

He raced to the big front door and pulled it open. A strong blast of fresh wind blew sand in his face! He screwed up his eyes and peered out in delight. The Castle had materialised on a lovely golden beach right next to what appeared to be – a holiday camp!

3
Duckling's Holiday Camp

Duckula ushered Igor and Nanny out of the Castle and slammed the front door behind him. He locked it and laid the heavy iron key under the mat.

They were now standing on soft, warm sand. The sun was shining brightly in a clear blue sky and the sea lapped gently at their feet. It was still early and the beach was deserted; no one had seen the Castle arrive.

'Beautiful!' declared Duckula, jumping up and down in excitement.

'Charmin'!' screeched Nanny, removing a shoe and dipping her toes into the water.

'Revolting!' said Igor, shielding his eyes from the sunlight. 'It's beyond me why we've come to such a dreadful place!'

'There's the reason,' replied Duckula, pointing to what looked like a town of dazzling white-roofed chalets, surrounded by a high, white stone wall. There was a big entrance gate, manned by two attendants – one tall and thin like a stork, the other shorter and fatter, like a penguin. Overhead there was a huge sign with letters painted in all different colours. It read:

Welcome To
DUCKLING'S HOLIDAY CAMP

The Transylvanian trio trudged along the beach to the entrance. Duckula went up and addressed the penguin-like attendant. 'Good morning, my dear fellow. Can you please direct me to the person in charge? I've come to apply for a job – and Igor and Nanny here are going to stay with me as guests.'

'*You'll* be all right, mate – there's plenty o' jobs goin',' answered the attendant. 'But your friends 'as 'ad their chips. We's full up, you see. Burstin' at the seams with holidaymakers.'

'Good, now we can *go!*' mumbled Igor under his breath.

'Did you say something?' demanded Duckula, annoyed.

'I said, "what a blow!", milord.'

'Well, there's only one thing for it . . .' said Duckula slowly.

'Return to the Castle?' ventured Igor.

'No, quite the opposite, Igor.' The Count smiled impishly. 'You and Nanny can work here *too!* Igor . . .? *Igor!*'

But Igor wasn't listening. He'd fallen flat on his back in a dead faint at this unexpected news.

It was a peculiar sight that passed by the window of the holiday camp manager's office shortly afterwards: a youngish duck in red bow-tie and cape, followed by a gigantic, clumsy chicken in apron and cap, carrying an unconscious, dark-suited butler effortlessly over her shoulder.

'Who are *they?!*' said the manager in alarm to Olivia, his secretary, who was busily filing her nails.

'They want to work here, Mr Duckling,' giggled

21

Olivia. 'Harry just rang from the front gate to warn us.'

'I suppose they *could* scare people in the Ghost Train!' smirked Mr Duckling. 'I think I'll go for a walk. Tell them I'm not available!'

Too late! Before he had time to sidle out of his office, his door burst open with a sickening crunch and Nanny stormed in – still with Igor thrown over her shoulder! She set him down in a chair opposite Mr Duckling's desk, then she sat down in another chair, which promptly collapsed under her weight.

Duckula entered sheepishly. 'Hello there!' he said, with a foolish expression. 'Sorry we came in without knocking. Sorry about the door. Sorry about the chair. Sorry about Nanny . . .'

The manager sank back in his leather chair. 'What is it you want?' he asked irritably.

'Three jobs, please!' requested Duckula hopefully.

'Ha, ha, ha! You come in here and break up my office and then ask me for jobs!' Mr Duckling stood up and walked to the window. He was tall with twinkling eyes, but he looked as if he could be bad-tempered too. 'Listen, buster, when I turn round, I expect you to be gone! One . . . two – hey, there's a big castle on the sands!'

'I know – that's where we live,' said Duckula sadly. 'It's not much, but we call it home . . .'

'What a wonderful place!' cried the manager, clapping his hands together. 'It would make a great new attraction for Duckling's!'

'It would?' gulped Duckula. 'I mean, yes, it *would!* Oh, it definitely would!'

22

'Funny, it's the first time I've noticed it – but these builders work so quickly nowadays, don't they? Fake turn-of-the-millenium, is it?'

'Yes, yes!' agreed Duckula, not understanding a word of what the manager was saying.

Mr Duckling was overjoyed at the idea of Castle Duckula as a crowd-puller. 'Now, about those jobs you mentioned . . .'

'Yes? You mean – '

'I think you'd make a *perfect* Yellowbeak! After all, you already have a yellow beak! Trouble is, I'm not so sure about your mum and dad here – '

'Hey, steady on – Igor and Nanny aren't my mum and dad!'

'Sorry, your grandma and grandad, then. No? Great-grandparents? Great-*great* grandparents . . .?'

Nanny stood up and towered over Mr Duckling. ''Ere, less of your cheek! We're not *that* blinkin' old, you know!' she squawked.

'Yes, you are, Nanny – and even older than that!' whispered Duckula. 'But that's beside the point!'

By now Igor had recovered sufficiently to speak. He rose to his feet, straightened his tie and addressed Mr Duckling.

'Allow me to explain. You are now in the presence of my lord and master – Count Duckula of Transylvania!'

'Oh, Count Duckula, eh? Ha, ha!'

'I am Igor, his butler and manservant – '

'Phoo-ee! Butler and manservant, eh? Ho, ho!'

'And this is milord's nanny – '

'Hmm . . . and, pray, what is she called?'

23

'I'm called Nanny, of course,' she squawked.

'How very original!'

Duckula was tiring of the wisecracks. 'Mr Duckling,' he shouted. 'Have we got a deal or not?'

'Okay, if you'll let me put your Castle in my adverts, I'll let you be a Yellowbeak, and your butler can buttle to his heart's content. But Nanny presents a problem. I mean, she's wearing a sling. Has she got a sore arm or something?'

'If you're incineratin' that I'm not capable of a good day's work – well you'd better bloomin' *not*, that's all!' shrilled Nanny.

'Nanny's sling is a *legend*, Mr Duckling,' added Duckula. 'She can produce anything you want out of it!'

'Oh, in that case, I'll have a cup of tea, please, Nanny,' grinned Mr Duckling sarcastically.

'Indian or China?' Nanny responded in a flash, bringing out four cups and saucers, milk and a sugar bowl and slapping them down on the table.

Mr Duckling's eyes bulged. 'Er – *any* sort . . .' he faltered.

'Right you are, Mr Ducklin'. I've got a pot freshly brewed!' And with a flourish Nanny pulled from her sling a big, steaming teapot and proceeded to pour out the drinks. Then she stopped and produced another cup and saucer. 'Whoops-a-daisy, I nearly forgot your secretary!'

Over tea, Mr Duckling became more friendly with the newcomers. He agreed that Duckula could be a Yellowbeak, supervising fun and games during the day and helping behind the scenes in the theatre during the evening shows. Igor was to wait on the guests in the dining room, and Nanny would be a chalet maid.

Mr Duckling said that he was short of time; he had a new helter-skelter to go and see. So he asked Olivia to take the new members of staff to their chalets. They all shook hands with him and left the office.

'This way,' said Olivia, waggling out of the office and leading Duckula, Igor and Nanny over the main drive of the camp.

As they crossed the roadway a big black car raced in through the entrance gate and screeched to a halt with an ear-splitting squealing of brakes and a prolonged blast on the horn. Igor and Olivia leapt to the far side of the road; Nanny and Igor jumped backwards.

'Road hog!' yelled Duckula.

But there was no apology from the driver, a large middle-aged hawk-like woman, wearing a fancy hat full of artificial flowers. She merely stuck her nose in the air as if she could smell rotten eggs, and moved the car off slowly.

'First lesson, Mr Duckula,' said Olivia, wagging her finger at him. 'Never be rude to the guests. They're here to have a good time!'

As the car passed by, Igor noticed that in the passenger seat was a younger woman – very pretty, with curly feathers on top of her head – who appeared to wink twice at Igor. He blushed and smiled feebly at Nanny, who had seen what had happened.

'Ooh, did you see *that*? The young flibbertygibbet!' she said in disgust.

Igor said nothing. He stood and stared after the disappearing car, flattered by the unexpected attention he had received.

'Come on, Mr Igor,' shouted Olivia, bringing him back to his senses.

She guided Duckula, Igor and Nanny through the camp, which consisted of a maze of little roads, lined with lots of beautiful little white chalets. There were plenty of people about: children playing and eating ice-creams; couples riding amazing cycles which seated two people side by side; grown-ups in swimming costumes and coloured shorts and T-shirts. And then Duckula spotted his first Yellowbeak – a tubby, smiling young fellow leading a crocodile of laughing youngsters who were copying the funny faces and silly movements made by their leader as they walked along.

Here and there between the chalets, Duckula glimpsed wonderful things like playgrounds, mini-funfairs, dodgem rides, amusement arcades, and an inviting paddling pool, packed with children who were splashing each other and screaming with delight.

'Isn't it *great?!*' cried Duckula, bubbling over with enthusiasm.

'If you *like* this sort of think, milord,' murmured Igor. 'Myself, I prefer the subtler pleasures in life . . . like a dark, damp underground room . . . with the incomparable aroma of fresh dry rot creeping through the timber work – '

'Stop it, Igor! I'm looking forward to my elevenses – and I won't be able to eat if you carry on talking like that!'

'How long do you expect we'll be here?' queried

26

Igor. 'I'm not looking forward to serving the public with their meals, you know. Not my scene at all, as they say.'

'Oh, we'll only be here for a few days,' said Duckula confidently. 'It can't take much longer than that for my extraordinary talents to be spotted.'

'And may I inquire what you intend to do about the Castle, sir? Have you forgotten that it will return home automatically at dawn, Eastern Transylvanian time? Leaving us stranded here – and Mr Duckling without an attraction for his holidaymakers.'

'The Castle!' Duckula slapped his hand on his forehead and looked extremely worried. Then he composed himself and coughed to give himself a moment to think. 'Ah, *yes* – didn't I tell you about the Castle?'

'You did not, milord.'

'Well, I'm telling you now. The Castle – the *Castle* will be fine! I'll nip back to it every day just before dawn and let it take me home. Then I'll simply bring it back here for another twenty-four hours. Now, what could be simpler than that?'

'A lot of things, sir, with respect,' groaned Igor.

'Here we are!' announced Olivia, stopping at three neat little chalets in a row. 'This is where you'll all be living while you're at Duckling's. Make yourselves at home – you'll be starting work this afternoon!'

4
Hard at Work!

Duckula was a Yellowbeak at last! During his first afternoon he worked flat out – and it left him *feeling* flat out!

First there had been the Grand Kite-Flying Competition on the playing field. Duckula had found it impossible to judge which child's kite had flown highest. The event ended in a scuffle between three boys and two girls, five broken kites and a horrendous muddle of strings which Duckula was quite unable to sort out. Finally he had brought about an uneasy peace by treating all the competitors to free Cornettos.

Then, long after the appointed time, he had had to race back to the ballroom to judge the Grandads' Knobbly Knees Contest. This event also turned into a minor disaster, when a squabble broke out between the first and second prizewinners as to whose knees were actually the knobbliest. Duckula was amazed by the ferocity of the argument and he wished he could have settled the dispute immediately by exhibiting Igor's knees, which he knew were by far the knobbliest this side of the solar system. Sadly, he hadn't been able to do this, as staff weren't allowed to take part in competitions!

After sneaking quietly out of the ballroom, leaving the contestants prodding each other angrily with rolled-up knobbly-knee certificates, Duckula headed for the beach for his final assignment of the afternoon – the Sandcastle-Building Spectacular!

'Boy, I'm famished!' he said, rubbing his rumbling tummy. 'Hope they have plenty of broccoli in the dining room at teatime!'

Waiting for him on the beach was a horde of eager youngsters, all armed with buckets and spades. When they saw him arrive, they jumped around him eagerly, pulling at his cape and shouting for him to make a start. A freckled litle boy even jumped up and tugged at his beak, shouting, 'It's *real!* All the other Yellow-beaks wear cardboard yellow ones – but his is for real!'

'Guess who won't be winning the contest, little boy!' hissed Duckula through a gritted beak. 'Get lost!'

He shooed the children away, rearranged his dishevelled clothing and smoothed down his ruffled feathers, then yelled, 'QUIET!' in his very loudest voice.

It worked – which surprised Duckula enormously. Feeling pleased with himself, he continued by directing the youngsters to each stand on a separate patch of sand.

'All ready?' he shouted, as they stood waiting for the signal to begin building. He pointed to Castle Duckula, which stood like an eyesore on the bright seaside scene. 'See the castle on the beach? I want you all to build little ones in sand – '

'Huh!' shouted a girl. 'I wanna make a *proper* castle – not a mouldy ol' ruin like that!'

Duckula grimaced at this cutting comment; but he had already learned fast during his short career as a

Yellowbeak to shrug off such remarks from his charges.

'You have fifteen minutes from . . . *now!*' he declared. 'And *I* have fifteen minutes to myself,' he sniggered, spying a vacant deckchair nearby.

But he was badly mistaken, for the fifteen minutes that followed were among the most hectic in his life! Castle-construction took second place to all-out war! Sand flew everywhere as half-built, promising-looking castles were dashed to the ground by rival builders. Sobbing victims came up to Duckula, begging for him to intervene.

The final straw came when he became the butt of a practical joke played upon him by a pair of conniving twins. One of them came up to Duckula, demanding that he should settle an argument.

The boy took him across a battlefield beach of demolished castles to a smooth strip of sand, where a beautiful replica of Castle Duckula stood.

'That's my brother's castle,' said the boy, pointing firstly to the magnificent construction. Then he pointed to the sprawling remains of a wrecked castle which stood alongside. 'But look what he's done to *mine!*'

'Dear me, that's awful!' said Duckula. 'You shouldn't have done that!'

The boy began to blubber. 'What are you going to do about it?'

Duckula blinked and wondered what action he should take. Being a Yellowbeak was proving to be harder than he had expected.

'I'm so sorry. I shouldn't have done such a terrible

30

thing,' piped up the other twin suddenly in a polite voice. Said the second boy politely. 'To make it fair, my castle should be kicked down to the ground, then we'll both start again from the beginning. Will you kick it, please, Mr Duckula?'

Duckula really didn't want to destroy such a magnificent effort. 'Well, I – I suppose I *could* – ' he began.

'Please!' Both twins implored him.

'Very well, if you insist.' Duckula swung his foot right back, paused and then booted the castle as hard as he could.

Bam! It was a trick! The boys had built the castle over a huge rock – as Duckula's foot had just discovered!

'Ye-owwwwweeee!' screamed the novice Yellow-beak in pain.

He hopped about on his good foot, cradling the injured one in his hands, whilst the two twins and the rest of the beach party screamed even louder – with laughter!

'You little monsters!' yelled Duckula.

But the more he complained, the louder his tormentors laughed. Duckula sat back on the sand and consulted his watch. 'Right, that's it! The Sandcastle Spectacular's over!'

'Who's won?' demanded one of the twins. 'You've got to give the prize to someone!'

Duckula surveyed the beach. 'What a shame! No one has completed a castle – so no one wins,' he announced gleefully. He turned to the twins. 'If only *your* castle was still standing, you would have taken the prize!'

'What was it?'

'A brand-new sports car!' smirked Duckula, striding bravely off the beach, trying not to wince in pain whenever his injured foot touched the ground. He was starving hungry and the dining room beckoned.

His progress was however impeded by another mishap, for just at that moment he felt a sharp blow on the head – and a small rusty nut fell to the ground.

'Ouch!' he cried, rubbing his crown. He picked up the missile and examined it. 'Tut! Never rains but it pours – and it's evidently pouring *nuts* at the moment!'

He glanced round to see if he could identify who had thrown it at him, but the children were all too far away. So he looked up to the sky – and there he saw an ancient biplane cruising along high in the clouds.

'Gee, it must be off that old plane,' he said. 'I just hope it wasn't holding the wings on!'

The nut had indeed dropped from the biplane! And it wasn't the first component to have worked loose and fallen off since the rickety old machine had taken to the air only a few minutes before!

In fact the whole aircraft was a mass of slack nuts and bolts flying in loose formation! With its huge double wings, open cockpit and wheezing, smoking piston engine, it looked just like a relic from the First World War – and, you guessed it, reader! – that's precisely what it was! And can you guess who was the pilot? No, not the Red Baron . . . not Amy Johnson . . . not Richard Branson: it was none other than the

32

intrepid, world famous vampire hunter – Dr Von Goosewing!

'Voops-a-daisy, nearly stalled her! More revs, I think!' he cackled over the throaty roar of the spitting aeroengine. 'Vot a lucky Von Gooseving I am! I haff zee freedom of zee skies . . . a beautiful day in zee glorious English countryside . . . und not a wampire in sight!'

In the cockpit behind Von Goosewing sat a burly, posh businessman in a smart pinstripe suit. He leaned forward and tapped his pilot on the shoulder. 'Hey, Goosebump – get on with the job I'm paying you for! I don't wanna stay up in this crate any longer than I can help!'

Von Goosewing nodded vigorously and gave him a thumbs-up sign. Then he put the old plane into a steep dive and swept low over Duckling's Holiday Camp.

Von Goosewing's passenger was none other than E. J. Eagle, the incredibly rich property developer. He leaned over the side of the plane and studied the layout of the camp as they flew over it.

'How was zat!' shouted Von Goosewing, taking the aircraft back up into the clouds.

'Fine!' replied his goggled passenger. 'Now take her back over the camp and we'll take some photographs. Have you brought a camera, like I told you to?'

'I haff done better zan zat, Mr E. J.!' replied Von Goosewing. 'Vhen you hired me, you didn't just get anybody – you got the legendary Dr Von Goosewing, inventor extraordinaire and, of course, celebrated

33

wampire hunter. No snapshotting wiz a liddle camera from me – I haff devised the amazing Gooseving Aero-Camera Mark I especially for zee trip. It comprises a cunningly concealed camera fitted beneath the fuselage of ziss aircraft. When I press ziss red button on my control panel, zee camera vill take a perfect set of photographs of Ducklink's!'

'Very clever,' agreed E. J., not at all impressed by Von Goosewing's enthusiasm; he'd spotted that the Aero-Camera Mark I was attached to the aeroplane with several rubber bands and two pieces of chewing gum. 'Get on with it man! I'm feeling airsick!' he rasped.

'Your vish iss mine command!' croaked Von Goosewing. 'I'll just do a loop-zee-loop to get into zee right position . . . zen ve'll svoop over Ducklink's und return to base.'

'You'll just do a *what*?' demanded E. J., straining to hear above the wind and engine noise.

'A loop-zee-loop!'

'You can't! I don't have a safety harness!'

But Von Goosewing was too busy with his manoeuvre to listen, and within a couple of seconds he was upside-down.

'Aargh! I shouldn't be doing ziss!' he cried suddenly. 'You don't haff a safety harness!'

There was no response from behind, so Von Goosewing turned round. E. J. had gone! Now Von Goosewing looked down and just caught sight of E. J. landing in the sea far below with a big splosh.

'Ach, he didn't like being up here anyway . . . but I vish he'd paid me in advance for zee petrol!'

Von Goosewing pushed his goggles over his forehead to see the cluster of instruments and switches in front of him. He put a finger over a large red button. 'May as vell complete zee assignment,' he murmured.

Then as he flew over Duckling's he pressed the button. But – you guessed it! – instead of taking pictures, something dreadful happened! The ancient machine gun burst into life, swinging from side to side and making a dreadful rat-tat-tat sound. Von Goosewing let go of the button but the rusty machine gun mechanism jammed and continued to fire. It shot the propeller to bits and the old biplane nosedived towards the ground!

'Drat, drat, drat! I forgot to rewire zee button to zee camera!' he screamed, pulling hard on the wobbly joystick, which came away in his hand. 'Vot a terrible day ziss has been! At least things can't get any vorse!'

Bleep, bleep! Bleep, bleep! An insistent high-pitched tone came from his wrist.

'Nein, nein! Impossible! Something vorse *has* happened! Mein ever-alert Wristwatch Wampireometer tells me there's a wampire nearby!'

Crash! Boom! Thud! Splat! The tired old aeroplane smashed into a thousand pieces on the sands of Bacteria-on-Sea!

Did the doctor survive? Ah, reader, you'll just have to wait and see! I suppose you're sitting on the edge of your chair, biting your nails in excitement, eh? What do you *mean* – you couldn't care less? You need a lesson in good manners from Nanny!

5

Food at Last

Nanny hadn't found her first day as a chalet maid very easy either! She'd felt foolish asking a holidaymaker where the stairs were, as she wanted to clean the bedrooms.

'Oh, dear, whatever sort of a place is it?' she'd asked.

'A bungalow!' the young man had replied.

'Bung a low *what*? Oh, I see, bung a low *roof* on, did they? What a bloomin' cheek! You should ask for some of your money back if they can't give you a proper chalet with an upstairs!'

She'd also been bitterly disappointed with the vacuum cleaner: as it didn't seem to pick up fluff at all well, she had abandoned it and cleaned out a row of sixteen chalets with a little dustpan and brush – before another chalet maid came along and showed her how to *plug in* the vacuum cleaner and switch it on!

But now she'd put her Duckling's apron aside for the day and took her place in the dining room in her usual apron. Fancy having a dining room in an apron! Oh, go on, reader, you know what I *mean*!

The dining room at Duckling's was a large hall filled with tables and chairs, at which mums and dads, children, babies and grannies were all tucking into their evening meal. It was a lively, cheerful atmosphere, noisy with the excited chatter of the diners and

36

the clatter of plates as the waiters and waitresses brought piping hot dishes to the diners. There was a delicious aroma of cooking food, which put a spring into Duckula's step when he entered.

He found the special tables reserved for the staff and espied Nanny at one. He almost *ran* over, delighted to see her, and sat down by her side.

'Ooh, Duckyboos, it's lovely to see you again!' beamed Nanny, stretching over to give him a big cuddle.

'Not *here*, Nanny! And please don't call me Duckyboos when people can hear!' Duckula pulled away quickly, embarrassed at seeing a group of his fellow Yellowbeaks nudging one another and smirking at another table.

'Just as you like, Duckyboos,' said Nanny flatly. 'Anyway, 'ave you enjoyed your first day 'ere? Lots o' fun an' games, I suppose?'

'Oh, it couldn't have been better, Nan! I've had a wonderful afternoon!' He tried to sound enthusiastic, even though he was fed up and his head was still throbbing from the impact of Von Gooosewing's fallen aeroplane component. He changed the subject. 'What about you, Nanny? How did you find your first day's work?'

'Oh, easy! I just went to the broom cupboard and there it was . . . me sweepin' brush, disinfectant, tin o' polish, fresh bed linen – '

'No, I mean . . . oh, never mind! When's the food coming? I'm famished!'

'Ooh, you'll laugh when I tell you, Duckyboos!'

37

cackled Nanny. 'It's waiter-service – an' guess who *our* waiter is! It's Mr Igor!'

'Really?' Duckula cheered up a little and rubbed his hands together. 'I should be okay for extra helpings of broccoli then!'

''Ere 'e comes now!' squawked Nanny. 'Oh, dear me, 'e still 'asn't mastered them swingin' doors!'

It was true! From the kitchen to the dining room, there were two doors, clearly marked IN and OUT. A French waiter, Marcel, laden with piles of dirty plates, cups and saucers, was heading for the kitchen. Just as he reached the IN door, it burst open the wrong way and Igor marched briskly out, knocking poor Marcel sideways. His crockery fell to the floor with a tremendous crash. This was immediately followed by a loud roar of approval from the diners!

Igor steadied himself and managed to hold on to a tray of meals that he was carrying.

'What a relief!' he boomed, without even an apology. 'At least I haven't dropped *my* tray!'

'Oh, yeah?!' growled Marcel, scrambling to his feet and brushing off scrambled egg and splodges of tomato ketchup. 'We'll soon see about *that*!'

Then he gave the underside of Igor's tray an almighty slap, throwing the tasty meals high into the air – and back down on to Igor's head.

Igor shook his beak to dislodge some mashed potato. He stood still for a moment, thinking of his beloved torture chamber back in the Castle, and of how he'd like to see Marcel stretched out on the rack and left to the mercy of the werewolf! But Igor was a butler through and through, and after several centuries in service, he knew how to control his temper. He merely picked up his tray and strode stiffly back into the kitchen – through the wrong door, of course.

'Boy!' said Duckula, annoyed at Igor's humiliation. 'You see that, Nanny? I've a good mind to – to give that other waiter a piece of my mind!'

'I shouldn't bother, young feller,' shrilled Nanny. 'It's Mr Igor's own fault. 'E's knocked the waiter over three times while I've been sittin' 'ere.'

Igor reappeared from the kitchen through the IN door but thankfully no collision took place on this occasion. As he trudged past, he nodded at Nanny and Duckula. 'Be with you in a moment, milord – and you, Nanny.'

Then he continued across to a table at the far end of the dining room. He had to pass a table at which sat the big lady who had almost run him over at the entrance. Next to her sat the younger lady – and there she was, winking at him again!

Igor blushed and stared hard. Yes, she sat with one eye opening and closing madly as she stared back at him. Igor was so distracted he didn't look where he was going. And what did he do? You guessed it – he bumped straight into Marcel, who promptly upset a jug of milk into a guest's lap.

'Why . . . you!' Marcel was furious. 'You are so beezy ogling the young lady over there, you bump me again! All afternoon you bump me! If you do it again – I will challenge you to a duel. So there!'

Marcel stuck his nose in the air and headed for the kitchen. In his temper, he made the mistake of using the OUT door, which, precisely on cue, was shoved open by a fast-moving waitress, knocking him to the floor once again!

'Can't you read, Marcel?' she snapped, stepping carefully over him.

'How very amusing!' sniggered Igor. He turned to Nanny and Duckula. 'Now, milord, dinner for two, is it?'

He snatched a menu from a nearby table and placed it in front of his fellow Transylvanians. Nanny took it and studied it for a few moments.

'Yes, Mr Igor, this'll do nicely – with a cup of 'ot chocolate, of course!' she declared.

'You don't just order the whole menu!' explained Duckula in amazement. 'You're supposed to choose *from* it!'

'But I thought you could 'ave as much to eat as you want 'ere, Duckyboos!'

'Well, yes . . . you can, within reason, Nanny. But – oh, never mind! Give her the lot, Igor.'

'Certainly. She *is* a hard-working girl, after all, milord!' Igor seemed almost genial. 'And for you, sir, I have been in consultation with the chef and arranged a special House of Duckula menu: broccoli soup, followed by cheesed broccoli served with extra broccoli, and, to finish, broccoli-flavoured ice-cream with a broccoli lollipop!'

'Gee, that's great, Igor – I'm starvng!'

'Shan't be a moment, sir.' Igor moved away to fetch the meals. He looked across at the winking young lady.

'Everything all right, madam?' he shouted in an oily

voice. 'I'm sorry I can't serve you personally. You're not at one of my tables.'

'Service with a smile, eh, Nan?' commented Duckula. 'Igor seems very pleased with himself!'

'Oh, you know why that is . . .' said Nanny.

'No. Why?'

'It's that young lady over there. Harriet Housemartin, she's called. Stayin' 'ere with 'er mother. Igor reckons she keeps winkin' at 'im!'

'Winking at Igor?! Are you serious, Nanny? Does she know he's about 648 years old?'

'Course she doesn't silly! Anyway, the thing is – don't tell Mr Igor – but I've noticed she winks when 'e's not even there. She winks all the time. I saw 'er in the pool earlier and she was winkin' as she was swimmin' along!'

'Hee, hee! Poor old Igor! Never mind, so long as it keeps him in a jolly mood!'

Now, reader, let's nip over to the Housemartins' table and listen in to their conversation . . .

'There's that dreadful old waiter again, Mummy. Why does he keep smiling at me?'

'I haven't a clue, Harriet, dear. He doesn't seem a bad old stick. Perhaps he's taken a liking to me!'

'Rather you than me, Mummy! I say – these contact lenses are really giving me a hard time. My eye's still watering.'

'Oh, yes, it's awfully funny, dear. It makes you look as if you're winking!'

Igor swept in with a trolley containing a feast for Nanny and Duckula. He smiled across the room at Harriet.

'Huh, there he goes again, Mummy,' she whispered. 'What a creep! He looks about 648 years old – and he dresses like an undertaker. Wouldn't surprise me if he was a vampire or something!'

'Oh, I don't know, Harriet. He's quite good-looking in an ugly sort of way!'

6

A Taste of Showbusiness!

Nanny's toil was over for the day, and, as soon as the last guest left the dining room, Igor's would be too. But Duckula still had the most exciting part of his schedule to come: the evening lay ahead, and that meant helping out with the show in the ballroom!

He arrived early and sat on a heap of old curtains backstage, looking round in awe at the lights, scenery and other paraphernalia that went to make up the evening's entertainment.

'Boy, this is it! I've arrived!' he said softly to himself.

'Glad to hear it!' giggled a voice from behind him. It was Molly, the head Yellowbeak, who compèred the show. She towered, stork-like, over Duckula, who thought she looked magnificent in her glittering jacket and matching top hat.

'Now, let's see,' she continued, 'you must be – '

'Duckula – er, Count Duckula!'

'What d'you mean – *count* you? There's only one of you, isn't there?' She smiled and whipped off her top hat. From it she produced a sheet of paper, which she handed over to Ducklula. 'This is your timetable for the night. It's easy . . . just open and close the curtains when it says so. Then you have to pass the comedian's disguises to him when he does his impressions. Oh, and finally you have to put the microphone on-stage for the singer. Got it?'

'Yes, I think so,' babbled Duckula.

'I'll be back soon. The show starts in fifteen minutes,' said Molly. Then, before walking off, she leaned forward and tweaked his beak. 'Hey, that's cute – a real yellow beak!'

Duckula walked on to the stage and peeked through a small hole in the curtains. The auditorium was filling up already with assorted holidaymakers.

Feeling safe in the darkness he bowed deeply, like a famous singer on the receiving end of enormous applause, and then held out his hand to acknowledge his imaginary band.

Now becoming even braver, he pulled from his pocket a small booklet which Nanny had given him. It was called *Songbook for Swingin' Transylvanians*. He turned to the first page, coughed to clear his throat, and began to sing, at first in a whisper and then louder and louder:

> 'Tran – syl – van – ia!
> It's the place for me – ee!
> Warmer than Lith – u – ania,
> Groovier than Hung – ary!
>
> 'Of all the lands I have seen,
> Transylvania is the tops!
> It's where my heart – '

'Oi! Who's making that racket?! How can oi rehearse me lines?' yelled a chirpy but friendly voice from offstage.

'Huh!' breathed Duckula, embarrassed at being

44

overheard. 'A *fine* start to my singing career, I must say!'

A short, fat fellow dressed in a shiny, baggy suit that looked as if he'd slept in it came out of the darkness.

'Who be you?' he demanded. 'Guests ain't allowed behind the scenes, you knows!'

'I'm not a guest . . . I'm a Yellowbeak, actually. Duckula's the name,' stammered the Count.

'Yeah? Why ain't you wearin' a yellow beak then? Whoops, sorry,' smiled the man. 'You *be* wearin' one!'

'I'm here to help out backstage,' explained Duckula. 'May I ask who you are?'

'Jackie Jackdaw at your service!' drawled the man in his strong West country accent. 'Comedian and star of the show!'

'Oh, Mr Jackdaw, eh? You don't look like a jackdaw!'

'Watch it, me duck! *Oi'll* do the jokes, if you don't mind!' He gave Duckula a friendly slap on the back.

Duckula took a liking to his new friend. He beamed and consulted his notes. 'Let me see . . . I have to pass you your funny hats and false beard and things when you're doing your impressions.'

'That's right,' nodded Jackie. 'And please make sure you gets 'em in the right order!'

'It goes without saying,' said Duckula, trying to impress Jackie with an efficient tone of voice. 'After all, Mr Jackdaw, I'm a professional!'

'Oh, you be in the business?'

45

'Yes . . . well, nearly . . . sort of almost. I intend to break into singing. That's why I'm working here.'

'Well, best o' luck, me duck! Oi hopes you gets what you wants. But you knows jobs in the camp is dodgy, don't you?'

'No. How d'you mean?'

'Well, poor ol' Mr Ducklin's very short o'money. The whole place be in danger o' closin' down!'

'But I thought the camp was full. The man at the gate said so!'

'Oh, Mr Ducklin' *pretends* the place is burstin' at the seams to make people want to come 'ere. Truth is, it's never more than 'alf full.'

'Oh, I didn't realise.'

'An' worse still,' continued Jackie. 'There be a millionaire property developer tryin' to buy the place for nex' to nothin' an' build a ferryport on the site. E. J. Eagle's 'is name; awful man, 'e be. Lives up at the mansion 'ouse in the town.'

'Gee, that's a shame!'

'Well, oi mus' be off to me dressin' room,' said Jackie brightly. 'It's curtain-up in five minutes. Break a leg!'

Charming, thought Duckula at this last remark. He didn't know that 'break a leg' is the traditional way of wishing luck to a fellow performer!

The evening was going well and Duckula was delighted with his first taste of showbusiness! He pulled hard on the ropes and managed to open and close the curtains right on cue.

The show had started with some lively music from

46

a band of four musicians. Then Molly the compère had come on to introduce a team of acrobats, with a clever line about tumblers being the things you got free when you bought four gallons of petrol; then, she'd joked, judging by their performance they *had* come free with petrol! Everyone had laughed – but actually the acrobats had turned out to be very clever. Duckula thought it was marvellous the way they could throw themselves all over the place and stand on top of one another until they reached right to the ceiling.

Now the audience was screaming with laughter as Jackie stood on stage and cracked joke after joke.

'What did the ghost give his wife for Christmas? A fright!' he quipped. 'What's yellow and green and very tough? A buttercup wearing a leather jacket!'

Then the stage lights dimmed and a bright spotlight was trained on Jackie. He contorted his face until he resembled a film monster – very much like Igor!

'Ladies and gentlemen,' he hooted in a spooky voice that made the audience go silent, 'it's time for a party in the dungeons of . . . Duckling's Castle!'

Now it happened that Igor was in the audience; he'd decided to while away some of his free evening in the darkness of the theatre and he'd invited Nanny to join him. He sat up straight at the mention of the word dungeons and watched with interest.

'Mmm, just my cup of tea, Nanny!' he purred, nudging his companion.

'What? Cup o' tea, did you say?' shrilled Nanny.

'Shhh!' said the people nearby.

'Very well, a nice cup o' tea it *is*!' she warbled in a slightly quieter voice.

Igor didn't notice her produce a teapot, cup and saucer from her sling. She balanced the cup on her knee and filled it with tea. The cup, I mean, *not* her knee! Then she held it out for Igor. But Jackie had just cracked a clever monster joke, which made Igor laugh and slap his knees; the trouble was, he also slapped the cup of tea – all over himself!

'Ouch!' he cried. 'What's all this?!'

'It's your cup o' tea, Mr Igor!'

'Tea? I don't want *tea* now, Nanny!'

'Ooh, please yourself!' shrieked Nanny.

'Shhh, you two – else I'll put in a complaint,' moaned a man sitting behind.

'All right, keep your beak on!' replied Nanny, turning round to him. 'It's Mr Igor's fault. I distinctly 'eard 'im mention a cup o' tea!'

By now Jackie was moving on to his impressions. He winked at Duckula in the wings to signal that he was ready to be handed his disguise props.

Duckula opened the basket containing a large assortment of wigs, moustaches, hats and spectacles, and then consulted his piece of paper, which told him the order in which he should have each item ready. Well, he *would* have consulted it, if someone hadn't opened the stage door and let in a strong gust of seaside wind!

It blew Duckula's paper right out of his hand! He tried to catch it, but it fluttered high in the air and then floated gently down to the floor right in front of the audience.

'Oh, no!' murmured Duckula. 'What'll I do now?'

But there was no time to wonder! Jackie was edging

towards Duckula, holding out his hand as he said to the audience, 'The party's going with the swing . . . ah, there's someone I recognise! Why, it's – '

Duckula closed his eyes and plunged his hand into the basket as if it were a lucky dip! He pulled out a selection of props, handed them to Jackie – and hoped for the best!

Jackie's face crumpled up as he quickly donned a bald-headed wig, a big ginger beard and a silly hat with flowers, apples and pears on it!

'Yes, it's . . . it's the Prime Minister!' he carried on as best he could, changing his voice to a perfect copy of the Prime Minister's.

The audience screamed with laughter, not at the skill of his impression but at the ridiculous mistake!

'Oh, and *there's* somebody else I know!' said Jackie, pulling off his disguise, throwing it offstage and holding out his hand for more props. 'Why, I'm sure I've seen him at the cinema – ' He hurriedly put on the new disguise that Duckula handed him. 'Yes, it's . . . Charlie Chaplin!'

Again the audience fell about laughing, because instead of portraying the legendary shabby little tramp, Jackie was now dressed like Sherlock Holmes in a deerstalker hat, with a large pipe in his mouth and a magnifying glass in his hand!

'Boy, what a shambles!' groaned Duckula. 'I don't suppose I'll ever work on the stage again!'

When Duckula finally closed the curtain on Jackie's act, he hurried into the auditorium and retrieved the precious piece of paper which listed his duties for the rest of the show.

He raced back to the stage, placed the microphone in the middle, and returned to the wings, just in time to open the curtains again for Molly, who announced the final act of the evening – singer Vince Vulture.

Duckula was enthralled by the singer's performance. Vince strode boldly onstage, the band began to play, and he launched into 'Sunshine, Strawberries and You', the song made famous by Nanny's idol, Frankie Fledgling! Duckula was sure he could hear Nanny's voice shrieking with delight in the audience. And he was right, of course!

He watched Vince sing a few more numbers and then decided he'd better go and apologise to Jackie Jackdaw.

He felt dreadful as he pushed open the dressing-room door and found Jackie getting ready to go home.

'Oh, it's you Mr Duckula!' said Jackie with a deadpan expression.

'Yes, I – er – I want to say I'm sorry about what happened out there tonight . . .' began Duckula.

'Sorry?! You may be sorry but oi'm not!' cried Jackie, his face breaking into a huge grin. 'Why, tonight oi got the loudest applause since oi started in the business! Mixing up the props was a great idea. That's the way oi'm going to do it from now on – with your assistance!'

Duckula opened his beak in amazement as the smiling Jackie Jackdaw took his hand, shook it vigorously up and down and then gave him a hearty slap on the back.

7
Rise and Shine!

Next morning the bats came out of the Castle clock early.

'Top of the morning to you, Dmitri,' said Sviatoslav. 'It's very fresh, don't you think?'

'My thoughts exactly, Sviatoslav,' agreed Dmitri. 'We're at the seaside, if I'm not mistaken.'

'Perfectly correct, my friend. Bacteria-on-Sea, I heard the duck say – wherever *that* is.'

'Ah, wouldn't it be nice to leave the clock for a while,' sighed Dmitri. 'To take a couple of little deckchairs on to the beach . . . laze in the sun a while . . . with plenty to eat . . .'

'Plenty to eat?' asked Sviatoslav.

'Of course, my friend! You *never* go short of food on the beach!'

'Why?'

'Because of all the sandwiches there! Get it? *Sand – which – is – there!*'

The bats collapsed in a fit of loud laughter.

'Hee, hee!' said Dmitri recovering momentarily and wiping the tears from his eyes. 'The old jokes are the best!'

'They *have* to be,' spluttered Sviatoslav. 'After all, they're the only ones we've got!'

High above the Castle in the clear blue morning sky a biplane zoomed into view from behind a cloud!

51

Readers who have been paying attention so far will realise who it was. For those of you with a brainpower rating of one Nanny – it was the celebrated Dr Von Goosewing, safe and well after his accident on the beach!

The plane swooped and soared like a graceful bird. Upon closer inspection you'd see all the patches and extensive welding Von Goosewing had had to carry out in order to make the old girl airworthy again. But then you probably wouldn't want to get that close anyway – not with old Goosey at the joystick!

'Here vee are again, Mr. E. J.! Duckling's straight ahead! By the vay, I'm zo sorry about zee ducking I gave you in zee sea yesterday . . . and I'm also zorry zat I crashed before I could operate zee camera; not zat it mattered – I discovered zat I had forgotten to put ein film in anyway! Ach, ach, ach! (Zat's not zee machine guns again, readers; it's "ha, ha, ha!" in mein native language.)'

'Cut the cackle, Goosegrease. Get photographing – get results!' came the short, sharp reply from E. J. Eagle in the cockpit behind.

'You can rely on me ziss time, boss!' Von Goosewing dived steeply towards the holiday camp below and placed his finger at the ready over the red button on his instrument panel. 'Chocks avay, old bean . . . bandits at ten o'clock!'

E. J. Eagle glanced at his watch. What was this loopy pilot talking about? he thought. Ten o'clock indeed! It was only just turned half past eight!

The roar of the engine was unbearable as the rickety old aeroplane skated low over Duckling's. Duckula's spoon rattled in the mug of cocoa that Nanny had made for him.

He was sitting at a small table with Igor and Nanny in her chalet, as the three of them prepared to face their second daunting day at Duckling's.

'Gee, that was low! The pilot must be a stuntman! I wouldn't mind taking a spin round the beach myself.'

'Ooh, you don't want to go up in no airyplane, Duckyboos!' squawked Nanny. 'Not without me to take care o' you anyhow!'

'If *you* were with me, Nanny, we'd never get airborne!' returned Duckula quickly.

'Cheeky young scallywag!'

Duckula yawned and rubbed his eyes.

'You still tired, Duckyboos?'

'Yes, Nanny, you can say that again!'

'Oh, all right – you still tired, Duckyboos?'

Duckula tutted and glanced across the table at Igor, who sat pensively with his heavy eyelids drooping as usual.

'Are you tired too, Igor?'

'Not particularly, milord. I'm bearing up. My duties here are much the same as at the Castle – except, of course, that I get paid on a regular weekly basis.' Igor laughed gently at his joke.

'Oh, we *are* on form this morning!' replied Duckula. 'Remember, Igor, no one is irreplaceable.'

'Ah, yes, sir, but I do have my uses . . . reminding you of the time, for instance.'

'Eh? What are you getting at?'

'Well, for example, it's fortunate I'm here to tell you that it's now almost a quarter to nine . . .'

'So?'

'That leaves you, milord, with precisely five minutes to reach the Castle before it returns home under its own steam . . .'

Whoosh! Duckula said nothing; he simply banged his cocoa on to the table and disappeared from the room at the speed of a greyhound.

As he streaked across the holiday camp and out through the gates towards the Castle, Von Goosewing's vampireometer went haywire on his wrist. He pulled his hand away from the red button, and shook his arm violently up and down – but the vampireometer continued to make a fast bleeping noise and its litle finger spun round and round on its dial.

'Ach, there it goes again! All zee indications are zat there iss ein dreaded wampire in zee vicinity! But how can it be? *Ziss* iss England, after all!'

'*Will* you get on with the aerial survey!' boomed E. J. Eagle down Von Goosewing's ear. 'Stop playing with your watch and start taking pictures!'

'I vould if I hadn't missed mine chance!' shouted back Von Goosewing. 'I'll have to circle round again and get back into position!'

E. J. Eagle shook his head in disbelief and held on to his churning stomach.

As Von Goosewing turned his flying crate, he noticed for the first time the Castle on the beach.

'Vot in Bavaria is *zat?*!' he cried, rubbing the glasses of his goggles in disbelief. 'It looks like ze notorious Castle Duckula! *Nein*, it cannot be . . . it must be von of zose seaside amusements or somethink . . .'

'What are you twittering about now?' demanded E. J.

'Zee castle down under, Mr E. J. I thought I recognised it!'

'Castle? There are no castles round here!' scoffed E. J. 'If there were, I'd have already converted 'em into hotels!'

'Vell, take a peek for yourself if you don't belief me!'

E. J. sat up in his seat and peered over the side of the aircraft. But he was too late, for it was now dawn, Eastern Transylvanian time and Castle Duckula had just dematerialised in a blaze of coloured, flashing light.

'There's nothing there – only *sand*, you birdbrain!' snapped E. J.

'Vot?!' Von Goosewing scanned the beach in vain. He leaned farther and farther out, neglecting to keep the joystick in a central position. So the aircraft slowly turned over – until it was completely upside-down!

'No, I see nothink!' burbled Von Goosewing. 'Oh, vait a moment, vot's zat? There's someone just like you, Mr Eagle, sir, falling through zee skies!'

There was no answer from behind. Then it dawned on Von Goosewing that they were flying upside-down – and E. J. still hadn't been wearing a safety harness!

'Nein, nein, nein! It can't haff happened *again!*' he screamed in dismay. 'Ziss isn't fair! I want mine mummy!'

Nanny was pleased that she had almost finished her early morning chore of making the beds in the rows of chalets for which she was responsible.

She arrived at the last one in a good humour, humming a little song that she used to sing Duckula to sleep with. Really it used to keep him awake, but she never knew!

She gave a little tap on the door and walked straight in. A huge soaking wet sponge, carefully balanced above the door, fell with a soggy plop on to her head and made her jump!

'Ha, ha! Ho, ho!' Two small twin boys ran out at high speed, screaming with delight, spinning Nanny round as they rushed past her.

'Bah! Children today!' she moaned, squeezing water out of the offending sponge and using it to mop her face and beak dry.

'Help!' came two timid voices from the bedroom. 'Help us!'

Ah, that's probably just another prank, thought Nanny! In order to carry out a surprise ambush, she crept up to the bedroom door, quietly turned the handle – and then gave an almighty push. Unfortunately the door was locked, but with Nanny's weight behind it, it just gave way and crashed to the floor with Nanny on top of it!

Nanny picked herself up, adjusted her sling and looked round in bewilderment. There were no children in the room: just an elderly grandma and grandad sitting up in bed.

'Thank goodness you've arrived, missus!' said the grandad, who was painfully thin and dressed in pyjamas and a daft nightcap.

'Yes, thank goodness,' repeated his frail wife, wearing a big nightie with Benidorm written across the front.

'Our naughty grandsons locked us in. We've been stuck here all morning,' volunteered the grandad shyly. 'I'm Mr Corncrake, by the way.'

'Yes, stuck here all morning,' repeated his wife again. 'I'm Mrs Corncrake, by the way.'

'An' I'm Nanny!' announced Nanny.

'Nanny *what?*' enquired Grandad Corncrake.

'Jus' Nanny, that's all!'

'You can't be just called Nanny,' said Mr Corncrake. 'Nobody's just called one name.'

'Nobody,' confirmed Grandma, shaking her head in a sad manner.

'Ooh, you've got me thinkin' now,' muttered Nanny, knitting her brow (the only successful knitting she *can* do!) and twisting her beak in a strange way. 'Nope! I've just been plain ol' Nanny for as long as I can remember.'

'Never mind, Nanny. I'm sorry you've been troubled,' said Grandad Corncrake in a kindly way. 'Them two young grandsons of ours are just too much to handle.'

'Too much to handle,' agreed Grandma.

'We've only been here for two days and we're totally exhausted with the merry dance they've been leading us.'

'Totally exhausted.'

'And we've nearly another two weeks to go. I honestly don't know how we shall manage.'

'Another two weeks . . .'

'You poor dears,' cooed Nanny. 'I know 'ow 'ard it can be seein' to young whippersnappers. I looks after one meself. Tell you what, ol' Nanny'll 'elp you to take care of 'em. I'll take 'em off your 'ands right now for a while – an' give you both a bit o' rest!'

'How wonderful . . . but are you sure?' asked Grandad.

'Are you sure?' repeated Grandma.

'I'm always as good as me word!' squawked Nanny. 'Don't you worry now – I'll bring them back at lunchtime!'

'Oh, thank you so much, Nanny!'

'Yes, thank you so much!'

'Think nothin' of it. Bye, now! See you later!' Nanny made to leave but then she turned back. 'Whoops, I nearly *forgot!*'

The Corncrakes were amazed at what happened next. Nanny bustled round and made the bed for them – whilst they were still in it! She tucked them in tightly, left them with a hot pot of tea and then set off to find the terrible twins.

8
Double Trouble

Remember Duckula? We left him running to the Castle to catch it before it returned by itself to Transylvania. Did he make it? Yes, but he got there only just in time!

No sooner had he collapsed breathlessly in a heap on the hall floor, than the Castle began to shake and shimmer and shudder – and then it vanished!

Back in Transylvania the village peasants groaned as they looked up and saw the Castle return to the jagged finger of rock which had been its home for centuries.

'Hecky thump!' said one sickeningly grubby peasant who was wearing a plastic bin liner because someone had pinched his best sack. 'The evil ones have returned; we're doomed!'

Imagine his surprise when, only moments later, the castle vibrated and radiated light and was quickly gone again! This was because Duckula, upon arrival, had immediately gone down to his control-centre coffin and sent the Castle whizzing back to Bacteria-on-Sea for another whacky twenty-four hours!

And now, in Duckling's, he was driving a train! Not a real one, you understand; it was more of a tractor with a wooden body disguising it as a locomotive, and it was pulling several carriages brightly painted with cartoon characters like Dangermouse and Penfold.

The carriages were filled with noisy children, giggling, shouting and devouring ice-creams and lollies. Despite the fact that some of the cheekier ones were yelling things like, 'Move up to second gear!' and, 'Have you still got the brakes on, mister?' Duckula was overjoyed to be chugging along the roadways past the rows of chalets.

He turned a corner and found Nanny and the Corncrake twins waving him to stop.

'Coo-eee, Duckyboos!' screamed Nanny. 'It's *me*, Duckyboos! Can we have a ride on your train?'

'Coo-eee, Duckyboos!' chorused the entire train of young passengers, delighted that they had discovered their driver's softie pet name.

Duckula went red with shame. He brought the train to a shuddering halt and jumped out.

'Ooh, thanks, Duckyboos!' shrieked Nanny again, totally unaware of the embarrassment she was causing.

'Ooh, thanks, Duckyboos!' mimicked the passengers again.

'Will you stop calling me . . . that name . . . in front of everyone!' demanded Duckula.

'What – Duckyboos, you mean?' asked Nanny, blinking.

'Shhh! Yes! Now get on board and let's get moving.' He eyed the twins standing with Nanny. 'Oh, no! It's you two! The sandcastle twins, eh?'

'No, they're called the Corncrake twins – not the Sandcastles,' Nanny told him.

Duckula ignored her. He decided to put the naughty pair at the back of his train where, hopefully, they would cause less trouble.

'Come on!' He signalled to Nanny and the twins to follow him to the rear. 'We're nearly full – but there are some seats in the last carriage.'

He opened the door and held out his hand to help Nanny and the boys aboard. Nanny stumbled on and so did one twin. But there was no sign of his brother.

'Where's Tom, Tim?' queried Nanny.

'*I'm* Tom, Nanny.'

'Well, where's Tim, Tom?'

'Search me. I'm not my brother's keeper!'

The answer soon came, for suddenly the train moved off with a jerk. Tim had evidently taken control of the engine!

Duckula began running to the front. His little legs went up and down like pistons and his cloak blew out horizontally behind him. But the train gathered speed and began to overtake him.

'Watch you don't take off!' cried an impish girl with red hair and freckles from the safety of her seat.

'Come on, Ducky-wucky-boos! You can do it!' yelled a boy with a juicy orange lolly that made Duckula feel parched.

It was no use. He was about to give up, when the final carriage came past him and Nanny's strong arm scooped him up and dropped him in the seat by her side.

'That *wicked* boy!' she screeched. 'Goodness knows where we'll end up . . . prob'ly in the swimmin' pool.'

'I *know!* I've got to save the train, Nan!' exclaimed Duckula in a panic. Then he had an idea. 'I've got it! I've got it!'

He climbed on to the roof of the carriage and then

clambered precariously along it on his hands and knees, as the train clattered on. It was just like being the hero in a cowboy film, he thought. Indeed, he felt like shouting, 'Yippee, I'm after you, you varmint!' but he kept quiet.

He jumped from one carriage to the next until he was sitting on the front one, looking down at Tim Corncrake. He gasped when he saw what was happening! Right in front of the engine was the camp's ice-cream seller riding his tricycle with a box on the front. He wasn't exactly *riding* – more pedalling for dear life to escape the train which was thundering after him and by now almost scraping his back mudguard! Worse still, only a few metres ahead lay a very solid-looking brick wall.

'Yipes!' cried Duckula. He jumped down beside Tim and nearly stood upon the footbrake, making the runaway train come screaming to a halt. He didn't quite make it, however, and the engine booted the tricycle up the wall, throwing ice-cream man and all his ices into the air!

Tim jumped from the driver's seat and lost himself in the crowd of children that leapt from the train and surged forward to help themselves to free ices. Duckula picked up the dazed ice-cream man and took an upturned tub of Raspberry Surprise from his head.

Then he spotted Tim sneaking off towards the funfair. He crept after him and grabbed him by the collar. 'Aha, got you!' he said triumphantly.

'But I'm *Tom!*' cried the boy. '*There's* Tim!'

He pointed to the other twin, who was approaching, firmly in the grip of Nanny.

"Ere's the guilty party, Duckyboos!' she announced. 'I jus' found 'im skulking round the back o' the ice-cream cart.'

'No, I'm *Tom*,' said her wriggling captive. 'Mr Duckula's got Tim.'

'Don't believe a word of it!' insisted the other. 'He's *Tim*, and I'm *Tom*.'

'Rubbish! *I'm* Tom – *he's* Tim!'

Duckula held up his hands in confusion, but Nanny seemed to have the answer. 'They're both wearin' identi-tickle jackets,' she observed. 'So I reckon they'll 'ave sewn-in name labels to avoid confusion. Let's 'ave a look!'

She turned back the collar she was clutching to reveal a little cloth tag which said Tim.

'So you're the culprit!' hissed Duckula.

The boy's face suddenly went red and he started to cry. 'It's not fair,' he wailed. 'I *am* Tom! Tim must have swapped jackets this morning without my knowing! He's always doing it to get me into trouble. Boo, hoo, I wanna go home!'

'Okay, okay! I can't stand to see people crying!' broke in Duckula, who was starting to sniffle himself at the youngster's outburst. 'Just forget it. But *please* – both of you – stop being so naughty!'

He released his captive, and Nanny let go of hers. The boys ran to each other's side and held hands, both grinning widely.

'Huh! Looks like we've been duped!' grumbled Duckula.

'Come on, me lads,' piped up Nanny. 'Let's find somethin' to keep you out o' mischief! I know, we'll go an' collect some pretty shells on the beach. If you put a shell to your ear, you can 'ear the sea, y'know . . .'

'You can hear it anyway when you're at the seaside!' chirped one of the twins. His brother giggled.

Nanny told Duckula she'd see him at lunchtime, then she set off for the beach with the two young outlaws trailing, not unwillingly, behind her.

'She's not a bad old stick, Tim!' said one.

'Hey, *you're* Tim – I'm *Tom!*' retorted the other.

Then they both began giggling uncontrollably – just like Sviatoslav and Dmitri in the Castle clock.

Soon Nanny and the young Corncrakes were walking along the shoreline. Nanny was engrossed in her search for nice shells, as she called them, but her assistants found it a rather dull occupation.

As they neared the pier, she stopped and picked up a particularly interesting specimen and put it to her ear in an effort to hear the sound of the sea – but all she succeeded in doing was to pour a quantity of salty water down her ear! She made a peculiar high-pitched scream and shivered. 'Ooh, that went right through me!'

'Never mind the shells – look what we've found,' said Tim – or was it Tom? – tugging at the hem of her apron and pulling her across to two water-skis lying almost submerged.

'Ooh, *them's* skis!' she declared proudly. 'Wonder what they're doin' 'ere? There's no snow in the summer. Come to think of it, there's no mountains either in Bacteria-on-Sea!'

'Oh, *skis*, are they?' said the twin, pretending he

didn't know. 'Tell me, Nanny, how – er – how would you go about wearing them?'

'Oh, that's easy! You jus' puts your feet in them loops! Look I'll show you . . .' She slipped off her red slippers and carefully inserted first one foot and then the other into the skis.

'Don't fall over, Nanny,' said the twin, faking concern. From the water he produced a wooden handle connected to a thin rope. 'Here, hang on to this to steady yourself!'

Vroom, vroom! The moment she grabbed hold of the handle with both hands, a powerful motorboat bobbing in the water nearby started up. The other twin – Tom, I think – was at the wheel. He cast off the mooring line and the boat started out to sea, quickly taking up the slack of the towing rope!

'This is 'ow you stands in skis,' Nanny was explaining. 'Then you jus' – aargh! Help me! What's 'appenin'?! I'm movin'!'

And moving she *was* – and at a fair rate of knots! All she had to do was to let go of the towing handle . . . but *you* know Nanny: she gripped even more tightly because she was scared! So she rose high in the water, skimming the choppy waves as the motorboat pulled her along faster and faster.

'Yaa – oohhh!' she yelled, twisting and turning in sheer fright. 'Heee-lp! Duckyboos! Mr Igor! *Anybody!*'

Sunbathers on the beach flocked to the water's edge to watch the amazing spectacle of what appeared to be a giant chicken doing expert tricks on water-skis! Nanny did it one-handed; she did it one-legged; and she even turned completely round in her attempts to shout for assistance!

'Bravo!' cheered an onlooker.

'What a woman!' hooted another.

'*What a ninny*!' sighed Duckula, watching her antics from the top of the Duckling's giant slide, where he was supervising the rides.

9

Duckula is Summoned

It was lunchtime at Duckling's – and Duckula's favourite time of the day! Except for every *other* mealtime, that is!

He sped into the dining room, thinking of broccoli, broccoli and more broccoli. If he'd been a lawyer, he thought, that's what he would have called his business: Broccoli, Broccoli and Broccoli!

He found Nanny at the usual table and took his seat.

'Oh, 'ello, Duckyboos!' she greeted him in a subdued voice.

'Hiya, Nan! I can smell something good cooking! What are you having – the whole menu again?'

'No, I'm not specially 'ungry this afternoon.'

'Really? How come? Oh, I see . . . you're feeling seasick, eh?'

'An' what d'you know about that?'

'I saw you water-skiing this morning. Bit of a surprise, I must say. Never thought of you as a pioneer of advanced skiing techniques!'

'I never bloomin' wanted to be. It was them blinkin' twins that put me up to it!'

'Never mind! You've got rid of them now, I take it?'

'Yes – but I'm picking them up again this afternoon. Grandma and Grandad Corncrake can't manage them!'

'Oh, *Nanny*,' smiled Duckula. 'You're too soft!'

Marcel the waiter waltzed up to them. He smiled and twisted one of the ends of his thin moustache. '*Bonjour, mes amis!* What may I do *pour vous?*'

'Banjo, did you say?' said Nanny. 'What you talkin' about?'

Duckula interrupted. 'And *bonjour* to you, Monsieur Marcel. What's happened to old Igor?'

'Ah, Monsieur Igor has – 'ow you say – swapped tables with me.'

'How's that?'

'Well, we 'ave agreed to a peace formula. 'E works on that side of the dining room and uses the IN door; I work on these tables and use the OUT door!'

'Oh . . . I see.'

'But confidentially, I believe your Monsieur Igor has another motive for swapping.' Marcel nudged Duckula and gave a knowing smile. 'It means he serves Mrs Housemartin and her daughter over there!'

Duckula and Nanny followed the nod of Marcel's head to a table, where the formidable Mrs Housemartin and her winking daughter were just about to sit down.

Igor came into view, lurching across the room to the Housemartins. 'Good day, ladies!' he boomed, pulling out the chairs, waiting for them to take their places, and then pushing the chairs forward again.

'Thank you,' said Harriet coolly.

'Yes, thank you so much! You're *very* kind!' beamed Mrs Housemartin, pleased at the courteous attention she was getting.

'I am Igor, your new waiter,' he announced with a

68

sickly grin, as he carefully adjusted the position of the cutlery on the table and then placed a menu in front of each of the ladies. 'Whilst you're choosing, I'll just check you have sufficient salt and pepper. Oh, dear, the pepperpot's only three-quarters full; I'll replace it right away!'

When he was out of earshot, grabbing a full pepperpot from another table, Harriet whispered to her mother, 'How did we get the creepy waiter? That nice French one was much better!'

'But this Igor chappie's such a *gentleman!*' laughed her mother, who had taken a liking to his elegant behaviour.

Igor returned with the pepperpot and began rearranging the cutlery again. He looked up again with a silly grin on his face. 'Now, what can I do for you?'

'You can stop messing with the knives and forks for a start!' said Harriet shortly, winking madly.

'Sorry, madam, I must say.' Igor drew back, confused. How strange! There she sat – winking at him and shouting at him at the same time.

'Ha, take no notice of my daughter, Igor,' said Mrs Housemartin nervously. 'She's grumpy because she can't get used to her new contact lenses.'

'That's perfectly all right, madam.'

'Look at her, poor girl, they make her eyes water, causing her to wink all the time!'

Igor's heart sank. So *that* was it! How disappointing – she wasn't winking at him at all! He didn't know what to say. He just stood there with his mouth open – a dumb waiter!

'Is there something the matter?' asked Mrs House-martin. 'You look a little drained. Well, you did *before*, but even more so now!'

'Er, no, madam. Nothing is wrong,' Igor coughed politely. 'Now, are you ready to order?'

'Yes, thank you. I'll have a cheese salad, please. I'm a vegetarian, you see.'

'Ugh!' whispered Igor. What a dreadful woman she must be!

'I beg your pardon?'

'I didn't say a word, madam. And you, miss?'

'A rare steak, please,' said Harriet.

'Right away, ladies!' Igor secretly licked his lips at the mention of steak. *My* kind of maiden, he thought. What a pity . . . oh, never mind!

'I think he likes me,' cooed Mrs Housemartin, when Igor had left for the kitchen. 'He's rather upper class, I must say. Quite different from most chaps we meet.'

'Yes, I think you can safely say *that!*' said Harriet. 'He looks like nothing on earth!'

'Don't be so awful, dear. I think he's quite cute. Shhh! He's coming back.'

Igor returned and dutifully placed the two meals before the diners. 'Thank you, ladies.'

'Thank you, Igor!' gushed Mrs Housemartin. 'Before you go, may I ask you what time you finish?'

'What time do I *finish*, madam?'

'Yes.'

'About two fifteen – then I'm free until around five. Why do you ask?'

70

'I wondered if you'd care to join me for an afternoon stroll on the promenade.'

Igor was aghast. 'Oh, I hardly think so, madam. I – er – omitted to mention the fact that I – er – '

'That you *what?*' demanded Mrs Housemartin, annoyed at being turned down. She was a woman who was rarely refused on any matter.

Igor had to think fast. 'I – er – can't stand strong sunlight.'

'Oh, it makes you feel poorly?'

'Something like that, madam.'

'Well, perhaps some other time, Igor,' rasped Mrs Housemartin. 'Perhaps when it's cloudy and dull!'

'Yes – perhaps, madam, perhaps.' Igor looked frantically for an excuse to make his escape. 'I must go, madam. My customers are awaiting me . . .'

Because she wasn't feeling too hungry, Nanny had ordered only half the menu for lunch, and Duckula was still ploughing into his plate of double broccoli with extra broccoli, when an unexpected guest joined them at the table. It was Mr Duckling himself.

'Hi! said Duckula. 'You eat here too? I thought you'd have had your own dining room.'

'No, I'm not eating,' said Mr Duckling. 'I've come to see *you*.'

'Oh, really?'

'Yes. Take a look at this!' He slapped a colourful poster on the table and unrolled it. 'What do you think of that?!'

The poster had a spooky sort of picture of Castle Duckula standing in mist and it was surrounded by

71

little pictures of people enjoying themselves in the holiday camp. At the top in giant letters it said:

COME TO DUCKLING'S
AND VISIT THE
GENUINE
TRANSYLVANIAN CASTLE
– IF YOU DARE!

'Wow, that's fantastic!' exclaimed Duckula. 'Look, Nanny, it's the Castle!'

'Ooh, that's nice, Mr Ducklin'.' She peered closely at the poster. 'What a lovely picture – it's better than the *real* Castle, isn't it, Duckyboos?'

'Unfortunately, yes,' agreed Duckula.

'Never mind,' said Mr Duckling cheerfully. 'Everything looks better in a photo than in real life!'

'Oh, in that case I'll replace Nanny with a giant-sized photograph!'

'Cheeky! Watch your manners!'

'I wouldn't want to mislead the public,' said Mr Duckling with a slightly worried look. 'You did say it was a *genuine* Transylvanian castle?'

'Yes, worse luck! Boy, what I'd give to live in an ordinary house . . .'

'I've organised a Grand Gala Day, starting tomorrow at ten o'clock on the beach,' went on Mr Duckling. 'There'll be a speech by me, lots of sandwiches, orangeade and balloons . . . then the public will be given a guided tour of the Castle – by *you*, if you don't mind – and then a free day in Duckling's.'

'Sounds terrific,' said Duckula, feeling exhausted at the very thought of it all.

'The publicity will be great for Duckling's. It should bring us loads of new visitors for the coming season. I really think your Castle will put Duckling's on the map!'

'It's already *on* the map!' exclaimed Nanny. 'I seen it in your brochure – a little red dot by the side of Bacteria-on-Sea.'

Mr Duckling smiled generously at Nanny. 'Good one, Nanny! You should be working with Jackie Jackdaw!'

She was puzzled by this remark but Duckula didn't take the trouble to put her right. He was more interested in Mr Duckling's plight. 'How is business, Mr Duckling?'

'Oh, fine, fine – but you can't miss the opportunity for a bit of public relations, can you?' He didn't sound very convincing.

'Good,' said Duckula. 'Only I heard a rumour that things weren't so hot. And then there's that property developer fellow . . .'

Mr Duckling's eyes swivelled shiftily as he tried unsuccessfully to hide the sad truth from Duckula. He was relieved when a timely interruption came along – in the shape of his secretary, Olivia.

'Hello, Mr D! So this is where you've been hiding out.' She nodded to Duckula and Nanny. 'Good afternoon. Hope you're enjoying working here!'

'I love it!' smiled Duckula.

'Yes, I like it too,' began Nanny, 'except for the wet sponge over the door . . . an' the train crash with

the ice-cream man . . . an' them bloomin' water-skis
. . . an' – '

Olivia was mystified; she wished she hadn't bothered to ask.

'What was it you wanted, Olivia?' asked Mr Duckling.

'Oh, yes, sir – I thought I'd better let you know as soon as possible. The star of our show can't make it this evening. He's had to go and see to his sick auntie in Yeovil.'

'Dear me!' exclaimed Mr Duckling. 'What can I do? How can I fill the spot at such short notice?!'

Duckula couldn't believe he was hearing this, his golden opportunity! Here was his chance to save the day by going on stage instead of Vince Vulture! Goodness knows *who* might see him – perhaps even a man from a talent show on television!

'Shall I ring the theatrical agency?' Olivia asked Mr Duckling.

'What? Oh, yes, I suppose you'll have to!'

'NO!' shouted Duckula so sternly that everyone went quiet. 'No need for that, Olivia. *I* will take over!'

'*You?!*' cried Olivia.

'*You?!*' cried Mr Duckling.

'*You?!*' cried Nanny.

'Well, don't *you* sound so surprised, Nanny!' said Duckula. 'I was counting on you for support.'

'Can you really do it?' asked Mr Duckling.

'Piece of cake!' purred Duckula.

'Cherry or sultana?' queried Nanny, delving deeply into her sling.

COMPLETELY BATS!

'Hee, hee, reader – this is Sviatoslav speaking! Dmitri and I have pinched three pages of this book for a little chapter of our very own! Trouble is, not much happens in the Castle clock – and, since the duck and his staff left for the holiday camp, nothing happens in the Castle either! Is it any wonder our humour is so corny?! Now I'll hand you over to Dmitri . . .'

'Hello, my friend! So kind of you to read our humble pages! Sviatoslav and I have put together a few holiday jokes for you. No, think nothing of it: if you've managed to get to the middle of this book, you deserve a break! Let's face it, *anything's* better than reading about Duckula and Co!'

'Hee, hee! Ha, ha! Ho, ho!'

Guest: Excuse me, there's a fly
           in my soup . . .
Landlady: Oh, sorry, sir – you're
           the vegetarian, aren't you!

What sort of fish comes in
all different flavours?
– Jellyfish!

Where do banshees go on holiday?
– To Wails!
How do they get there?
– On the Ghost Train!

Guest: Can I have burnt bacon with
           an undercooked egg, two
           slices of stale bread . . . and
           a cup of cold tea?
Landlady: I can't do all that for you!
Guest: Why not? That's what you gave
           me yesterday without my
           even *asking!*

A boat moored in Bacteria Bay
has a rope-ladder over the side
with the bottom rung just touching
the water. If the rungs are 25 centimetres
apart and the tide is rising 1 metre
every hour, how many rungs will be
underwater after 1 ½ hours?
The same as before, because the boat
will rise with the tide!

Why did the seaside landlady lock the
door on the bookmaker?
– Because he came in at ten to one!

Why do vampires wear black braces?
– To hold up their trousers!

You're driving a coach with 15 passengers to Bacteria-on-Sea. On the way you stop to pick up 20 more and drop 11 off. At the next stop 15 more get on and 10 get off.
What is the name of the bus driver?

It's *your* name. You are the bus driver, remember!

What lies on the ocean bed and shakes?
– A nervous wreck!

What do you call a man who
lives on the beach?
– Sandy

What do you call a bird with
a big beak?
– Bill

'That's all for now! Don't forget to laugh a little louder at our jokes next time you see us on television and, who knows, they might give us a bigger part in the show!
See you around!

SVIATOSLAV   DMITRI

10

An Afternoon Off

You can guess what Duckula did for most of the afternoon! You *can't?* Oh, I see, you've let those silly bats take your mind off the story with their potty jokes!

Well, Duckula practised his singing for his debut as the star of the show that evening. Igor sat with Nanny in her chalet, enjoying a well-earned rest and cup of cocoa – and listening to the master warble to the end of a Frankie Fledgling song next door:

> 'Sunshine . . . sunshine . . . sunshine,
> Sunshine, strawberries – and yo – ou – ou.'

None of us likes earache, do we? So let's stay with Nanny and Igor!

'Duckyboos sounds lovely, doesn't he, Mr Igor,' said Nanny. 'I'm glad I found 'im that ol' Transylvanian songbook!'

'Far be it for me to criticise, Nanny,' replied Igor, 'but I wonder if those tunes are quite the thing for a cabaret evening. I fear they lack that certain . . . sophistication . . . that today's audience expects.'

'Ooh, I don't know about that,' squawked Nanny.

'You don't know much about *anything*. That's my point.'

''E'll be all right, will Duckyboos. 'E's throwin' in

a few Frankie Fledglin' numbers as well, like that one 'e's jus' sung. They'll love 'im! Nobody could go wrong with Frankie's songs!'

'I hope you're right, Nanny,' said Igor, stirring his cocoa furiously to get rid of the lumps.

A knock came at the door.

'I'll get it, Nanny.' Igor stood up, walked across to the door and opened it.

Crash! Bang! Clatter! An enormous pile of sweeping brushes, mops, buckets, and feather dusters on sticks fell on Igor, knocking him to the ground. They had been placed against the door by the pesky Corncrake twins, who could be heard laughing as they ran away.

Everything went dark for Igor: he had a heavy metal bucket on his head!

Nanny rushed across to help him. She tried to dislodge the bucket but found it was too firmly jammed on.

'It's stuck, Mr Igor!'

'I can see that! Get it off me!'

'Ooh, you sound jus' like a robot! Your voice is all tinny!'

'*Will* you get this thing off!' boomed Igor.

'Don't worry, I'll 'ave it off you in a jiffy!' Nanny broke into a helpless fit of screechy giggling. 'Oh, you – do look funny, Mr Igor! Hee, hee, hee! 'Ave a look at yourself in the mirror! Oh, I'm sorry, you can't, can you! Ho, ho! Ha, ha!'

'Take control of yourself, woman,' growled Igor like an alien. 'Pull it off!'

Nanny helped him to his feet and got his head – his bucket, rather – under her arm. Then she pulled him

79

all round the chalet, causing him to stumble and bump into every piece of furniture in turn!

'Stop it!' he cried. 'You're dragging my beak off!'

She stopped pulling and told him to sit down. She had an idea, she said.

Igor sat waiting, wondering what trick Nanny had up her sleeve – or her sling! He didn't object to the darkness of the bucket, but this was a ridiculous, humiliating situation.

Bong! Bong! Bong! Igor's head started to vibrate and throb as Nanny bashed the bucket with the heavy end of a sweeping brush.

'This should knock it loose!' she cried.

'If it doesn't knock my brains loose first.'

'What brains are those, Mr Igor?' Nanny beamed with delight. It was the first time in centuries that she'd got the better of the grouchy butler!

'Butter, Nanny! Get some butter and I'll push it up inside the bucket.'

'Right you are, Mr Igor. Shan't be long!'

He listened to her leaving the chalet and then sat fuming at his predicament and listening to Duckula wailing next door. Wait till he got his hands on those brats!

Then another knock came at the door. Back again with another prank, were they? Right, they were in for a shock: he'd give them a piece of his mind, bucket or no bucket!

He fumbled his way to the door, snatched it open and stuck his bucket outside. He couldn't see, of course, that it was Mrs Housemartin and Harriet who were standing there.

'Clear off, you pair of pests!' he bellowed. 'If I catch sight of you two again, I'll – I'll stretch you on the rack in the dungeon!'

'Dear me, the poor man needs a lesson in etiquette – and I thought he was a gentleman!' sniffed Mrs Housemartin haughtily.

'Who's that?' Igor cocked his bucket to one side in order to hear better.

'It's Mrs Housemartin, you rude man!' She poked his bucket with the end of her umbrella. 'I don't know why you have to wear that stupid bucket on your head now the sun's gone in. I came to see if you wanted to join me on the promenade. Well, do you? Do you? Come on, man, give me an answer!'

Inside his miniature prison Igor groaned. Why on earth had the master brought him to this place? Why couldn't Count Duckula behave like a perfectly normal vampire, resting by day and stalking the Transylvanian Alps by night? Why is steak so expensive, and garlic so cheap? Why do the stars twinkle at night? Why was Nanny taking so long to get the butter . . .?

Nanny set off to fetch a packet of butter from the dining room kitchen but her attention was diverted by a shout from the bingo hall.

'Come on, gorgeous! Vee just want one more person and zen vee can start zee game!'

Nanny looked round to see who was calling – *and* if they were calling her.

'Yeah, I mean *you*, darlink! Come und make zee

numbers up! First prize ist ein wunderbar carriage clock!'

Have you sussed it, reader? Have you spotted that the bingo-caller is none other than the fiendishly devious Dr Von Goosewing, ingeniously disguised in an open-necked shirt and jeans as a lively showman with a cheeky line in chat?

Ooh, I loves a good game o' bingo, thought Nanny. I'll just have one go – it'll only take a minute! She sat down carefully on the one remaining empty high stool in front of a bingo card with plastic shutters that you pushed across when your number was up!

'Zat's zee ticket!' laughed Von Goosewing. 'You 'ere wiz your boyfriend, miss? Vot a pity! Right, ladies und gentlemen, off vee go for a full house!'

Von Goosewing started up the machine that blew the numbered ping-pong balls around, and then he began calling: 'On zee blue, five und two – fifty-three! On zee red, lucky for some – number eight! Kelly's eye – number six! On zee pension, six und five – thirty-two! Two liddle ducks – twenty-seven!'

'What's he up to?' yelled a woman.

'Gerroff!' cried another.

'You will please be quiet, everyone!' shouted Von Goosewing. 'How can I call zee numbers wiz such a racket going on?! When you behave, vee will continue . . . zat's better! Now, all zee fours – vierundvierzig, top of zee shop – neunzig . . .'

The players got up and abandoned the game, hurling abuse at Von Goosewing and raspberrying at him.

'Zame to *you*, you peasants!' he cackled. Then he began to mumble to himself. 'Little do zey know zat zee bingo game was merely a cunning ruse to infiltrate Duckling's, zo zat I can investigate any wampire activity here. Und I haff seen enough already: zee big maiden waddling tovards zee dining room is Nanny, the wretched servant of zat unspeakable terror of Transylvania – Count Dugula!'

Meanwhile – as they say in all the best stories! – back at the chalet another knock came at the door. Igor, still with his bonce encased in best quality galvanised steel, leapt to the door again, opened it and growled, 'Prepare to meet thy doom!'

'Charmed, I'm sure!' came Duckula's voice. 'If you speak to me like that, Igor, I'll have seriously to consider reducing your salary!'

'My humblest apologies, milord. I thought you were somebody else – *two* other people, in fact.'

'I know I'm pretty magnificent – but I've never been mistaken for *two* people!' joked Duckula. 'Hey, I suppose it's a silly question, but why do you have a bucket on your head?'

'It's a long story, sir . . .'

'You're awfully muffled, Igor. I know. I'll whip the bucket off so that I can hear you properly!'

He grasped the bucket, gave it a little twist and pulled it clean off without any effort.

'However did you manage *that?*' asked a red-faced Igor, shaking his head feathers straight.

'Honestly, Igor, what would you do without me?!' laughed Duckula. 'Look, it's an oval-shaped bucket – so a little turn sideways was all it needed to clear your beak!'

'And I've been sitting here for half an hour like a . . . *ninny!*' Igor exploded. 'Why didn't Nanny think of that?'

'Ah, that little word "think", Igor . . .'

'Yes, yes, I know, sir! Not a word that one associates with Nanny at the best of times!' Igor caught sight of the Corncrake boys peeping in at the door. 'Excuse me, milord, I have a spot of revenge to take.'

He charged through the doorway – and crashed straight into Nanny, carrying a block of dripping, melting butter! Now, especially for any scientifically minded readers keen on the theories propounded by Albert Einstein or Sir Isaac Newton, here's a new one: a mass in motion is stopped dead when it meets a mass like Nanny!

'Oof!' was all Igor could say, sliding down the front of Nanny's apron.

'Ooh, get your beak out of me pinny! Are you chasin' me twins?' moaned Nanny. 'An' why did you let me go an' fetch all this butter when you've already got your bucket off?'

Igor was still too winded to reply.

'Tom! Tim! Come with Nanny – we're off to the funfair!' called Nanny.

'Huh! Whose Nanny does she think she is?' exclaimed Duckula in a huff.

Igor, now recovered enough to walk, struggled through the open doorway of the chalet – and then did a somersault as he slipped on the big lump of butter that Nanny had dropped!

11
The Big Night!

Duckula's stage debut was getting close and he had butterflies in his stomach, together with a large quantity of broccoli, which now he dearly wished he hadn't eaten!

Being in showbiz was tough, he realised. After dashing from the judging of the Miss Duckling Beauty Contest by the swimming pool, he'd just had time to grab a late snack from a kind lady who'd been washing up the dishes in the kitchen, and then dash to the ballroom.

He arrived out of breath and ran backstage. Brian, another young Yellowbeak, was working the curtains.

'Phew, I'm late!' panted Duckula.

'Oh, you're okay,' said Brian. 'The acrobats are still on. You've got plenty of time to get your breath back.'

Duckula decided to wait in the wings and watch Jackie Jackdaw do his act – and then it would be time for *him* to go on in place of Vince Vulture!

The acrobats finished their clever tricks and bounded off the stage to a loud roar of applause. Duckula clapped too, and he heard someone else clapping behind him. He turned to discover that it was – Vince Vulture!

'Mr Vulture, what are *you* doing here?' he gasped.

'Why, my act, of course!' Vince smiled and displayed two rows of perfect, gleaming white teeth. 'After *you've* been on, that is!'

Molly joined them. She gave Duckula a peck on the cheek and wished him good luck. 'You're on next!' she smiled.

'B – but there must be some mistake!' cried Duckula, his legs trembling. 'It's Jackie Jackdaw now, followed by me instead of Mr Vulture!'

'Jackie's not here – he's visiting his aunt in Yeovil,' said Molly.

'But Olivia told me I was replacing the star of the show – that's Mr Vulture, surely!' Duckula was in a desperate state.

'Oh, I see what's happened. Let me explain. Jackie's the star of our show; he's *got* to be – he's been with us for the past twenty years. But Vince is our *Guest Star of the Week*!'

Duckula tried to gulp but his throat was too dry to do so. 'What am I going to do? I can't tell jokes!'

'Course you can. You'll slay 'em when you go out there!' said Molly encouragingly. 'Tell you what, I'll give you a good build-up! Hurry up now – don't let Duckling's down!'

Molly swept on stage and addressed the audience. 'Thank you, thank you! Weren't they wonderful acrobats? Now it's time for a great new act who's making his debut tonight here at Duckling's. He's the funniest comedian around . . . he's the funniest looking comedian around . . . he's . . . Count Duckulahhh!'

The audience clapped and cheered. Duckula wished he'd never been born!

'Go on, mate – walking on is the worst part!' said

Brian, placing a microphone in his hand and giving him a gentle shove.

Duckula felt as if he were stepping on cotton-wool as he went out there, accompanied by a few bars of cheerful music from the band.

There he stood, on the edge of fame and fortune, with hundreds of people watching him – but he didn't have a clue what to do! He didn't have a single joke prepared, yet he couldn't just stand there and make a complete fool of himself.

'Good evening, ladies and gentlemen – and the rest of you!' he began nervously, clutching the microphone for comfort. 'It's super to be here tonight! Have you heard the one about . . . about the – er – the little boy who said, "Mum! Every week I hand in my school fun money to the teacher, but we've never had any fun yet!" Ha, ha! He didn't realise it was school *fun-d*!'

There was a polite ripple of laughter from the audience but it was obvious they didn't think too highly of the joke.

'Um – I went to a horror movie the other day. It was terrible: I saw this awful creature with a big green face, big drooping eyes and a terrible cackling laugh – and *that* was only the man in the ticket-office!' More like *Igor*, Duckula thought, as he waited for laughter that never came.

'And have you been to – to the shops lately?' he faltered. 'Prices are sky-high. I asked for some batteries for my radio-cassette . . . and the man behind the counter gave me a mortgage application form to fill in!'

I'm making a real mess of this, Duckula thought.

They're going to start booing in a minute! He made a brave decision to confess to the audience that he wasn't a real comedian and explain what had happened.

'You're probably all wondering how I came to be here tonight instead of Jackie Jackdaw!' he began. 'It all started yesterday when I started work as a Yellow-beak. Boy, what a time I've had . . .'

He went on to tell them about his troubles at the Kite-Flying Competition and how there had nearly been a bust-up at the Grandads' Knobbly Knees Contest. He told them about the trick the children had played on him in the Sandcastle Building Spectacular and how a nut had fallen from a passing aeroplane and landed on his head!

Duckula was telling them a sorry tale – but the audience loved it! They began to roar with laughter! Duckula was puzzled at first, as he didn't intend to be funny. But when he sensed what was happening, he carried on!

He told them about the way Nanny kept calling him Duckyboos in front of strangers and how she ended up water-skiing against her will. He told them about the train crash with the ice-cream man and how he almost missed the Castle going back home to Transylvania. And of Igor's mishaps with the IN and OUT doors in the dining room.

The audience couldn't get enough of Duckula! He glowed with confidence at his newly discovered talent for making people laugh.

He related the tale of how Igor had sat with a bucket

stuck on his head for half an hour. 'I had to do *something*,' he joked. 'I mean, the bucket was *needed*!'

Duckula had stumbled upon the secret of success! Just being himself was far funnier than trotting out corny jokes. The audience didn't believe this jolly little fellow, dressed so strangely in red bow-tie and cape, was a real count, or that he really had a nanny or a butler or a flying Castle: they thought it was all just a part of his comedy act – and they loved it!

Finally, Duckula had to bring his act to a close. He'd been on for far longer than he should have been, and he could see Molly's smiling face in the wings, beckoning him to come off.

And when he *did* walk off, the audience went wild, standing up to clap and cheer and shout for more! Molly gently pushed him back on-stage for three extra bows.

Vince Vulture was standing by to go on. He gave Duckula a thumbs-up sign and flashed his sparkling smile. He also looked a bit peeved, Duckula thought.

Mr Duckling was waiting too. 'That was superb, Count!' he cried. 'Never seen anything like it. I know what *you'll* be doing at Duckling's in future!'

Duckula received more congratulations from Brian and other members of the stage staff and left by the stage door.

He heard a voice shout, 'Here he comes!' and then he was surrounded by a large group of fans, clamouring for his autograph!

'Sign this, please!' said a young man, thrusting a leg in a plaster cast at Duckula, who did as he was directed.

'Put "With Love to Henrietta"!' demanded an elderly lady, holding out a programme for him to sign.

After writing his name about twenty times, he thanked his new fans for watching and then skipped off, with a lovely bubbly feeling inside, back to his chalet.

'Gee, showbusiness is great!' he shouted at the top of his voice.

Waiting inside his chalet were Igor and Nanny – and a mug of steaming cocoa with chocolately bits floating on top.

Nanny gave him a big hug. 'Ooh, Duckyboos, me an' Mr Igor was watchin' the show. Everyone was goin' mad! I didn't understand why they laughed about the bits you said about me. I'm not funny, am I?'

Igor, too, was smiling. 'Congratulations, milord. Capital performance. You really *wowed 'em*, I think is the expression one would use nowadays!'

Boy, thought Duckula, life at Duckling's just won't be the same any more!

And he didn't know how *right* he was!

12
A Ride Into Town

Duckula slept soundly that night and was still snoring loudly next morning at eight o'clock, when Nanny went into his chalet with a mug of cocoa for him.

'Aw, 'e looks jus' like a baby!' she cooed, standing over him with an adoring smile. 'Best not to wake 'im, the little darlin'. I'll let 'im 'ave a lie-in!'

Lovingly she tucked the sheets round him and then tiptoed back out of the chalet. As she closed the door quietly behind her, she found the camp train, without its carriages, pulling up outside.

'Ach, hello there, sveetheart!' said the driver – Von Goosewing, still posing as a cheeky bingo-caller! He kept polishing the steering wheel with his handkerchief and chattered away in a guilty sort of way, as if he were trying to justify his presence. 'Dum-di-dum . . . I'm just tickling zee carburettor und varming up zee liddle engine for zee day. Zen it's back to zee old bingo hall for a hard day's vork. Vot a life, eh? I'm alvays on zee go! Neffer ein dull moment!'

Nanny nodded a greeting to him, took a big swig of Duckula's unwanted cocoa and returned to her own chalet.

'Gee vhizz, zat was one close shave!' sighed Von Goosewing, taking to the controls of the engine again. 'Ziss sure iss ein tricky assignment. But vhen you're zee world's greatest living wampire hunter, you zimply take danger in your stride!'

He did a clumsy fifteen-point turn and reversed the engine up to the front door of Duckula's chalet! Then he jumped down and attached one end of a coil of rope to the back bumper. He crept silently into the chalet and attached the other end of the rope to the iron framework at the foot of Duckula's bed!

Then he returned to the driver's seat and moved the engine slowly away, pulling the snoozing Duckula and his bed through the doorway and along the roadway past the rows of chalets!

'Good job zee beds are on castors!' cackled Von Goosewing as he approached the main entrance of the camp.

He was pleased to find the two security guards in their hut, sitting with their feet up and reading newspapers with outstretched arms, which prevented them from seeing the train with its unusual trailer gliding out through the open gateway!

Once on the wide, deserted road, Von Goosewing put his foot down on the accelerator and changed from a snail's pace to – well, about as fast as an old steam-roller!

'Ziss ist ein great day for mankind!' chortled Von Goosewing, glancing round to observe his sleeping victim cruising along behind. 'I'm taking zee fiend to mine boarding house, where there iss a surprise awaiting him! Not a cute liddle ornament made from seashells; not a novelty mug wiz "Duckyboos" on zee side: no, it's zee Von Gooseving Wampire-Waporiser Mark VI wiz Proton Destabilisation Booster. It's zee most adwanced, bang-up-to-date, state-of-zee-art device in existence; I know zat – because I only built it last night – just for mine liddle friend Dugula here!'

The train trundled away from the seaside, past houses and shops and into the town centre of Bacteria. Postmen, milkmen and people going to work were amazed to see the colourful engine towing a bed, in which lay a sleeping Transylvanian aristocrat in his best woolly pyjamas! They presumed it must be part of an advertising gimmick to herald the arrival of a circus or something of that nature.

'Nearly there now!' chuckled Von Goosewing, starting up a steep hill lined with terraced houses painted brightly in all sorts of different colours. Most of them were boarding houses, and the one in which Von Goosewing was staying stood at the top of the hill.

The engine chugged and coughed and spat out smoke with the extra strain of climbing up the incline. Von Goosewing patted it affectionately.

'Don't let me down now, liddle beauty! It's not zee end of zee line for *you*, but it *is* zee end of zee line for zee dratted Dugula! Togezzer, ve are making history!'

Now, reader, you may not believe that machinery has feelings; you may laugh at the suggestion that the Duckling's engine chose not to take Duckula to his doom . . . but nevertheless something very odd happened.

A flash of fierce flame streaked from the exhaust pipe at the back, followd by another and then another! The tow rope began to blacken and char. More flames came – and the rope caught fire.

Halfway up the hill the rope burned through and snapped. Without its load, the engine had a new lease of life and it spurted with renewed vigour up the incline.

'Wunderbar! I'm proud of you, mine baby!' cried Von Goosewing, flapping his arms around manically, as if he were conducting an invisible orchestra.

He stopped outside his dilapidated hotel on the brow of the hill, pulled on the brake lever, and jumped down to the back of the engine.

'Aaaaargh! Where has zee evil creature gone?' he screamed, kicking out at the engine. 'You stupid locomotive, can't you manage to pull a bed wiz a weedy liddle wampire in it?'

The engine didn't answer, of course. Instead it shot out a final blast of flame, setting fire to the bottoms of Von Goosewing's baggy trouser legs.

Cursing and shouting, he ran into the hotel, stood in the bath and switched on both taps to put out the fire!

And Duckula? When the rope had snapped, he rolled back down the hill and into the town – without even waking up. Miraculously he didn't collide with any cars or land in a fountain or anything like that. He simply came to rest on a grassy field in a park. And he *still* slept on!

It was a few minutes before a park policeman came along and spotted him. He studied Duckula for a while and scratched his helmet. Then he took off his helmet and scratched his *head*.

'Excuse me,' he said finally, prodding Duckula to wake him. 'I've found people spending the night on a park bench but I've never heard of anyone bringing their own *bed!*'

Duckula sat up with a start. 'Where am I?'

'Wigglesworth Park.'

'Where's that? What am I doing here? I must get to the Castle before it disappears! What time is it?'

'Just turned eight-thirty.'

'Eight-thirty? I gotta go!' cried Duckula, throwing back the bedclothes and leaping out of bed. 'Quick, point me in the direction of Duckling's Holiday Camp!'

'It's *that* way,' said the baffled policeman, pointing up the road.

'Thank you officer!' cried Duckula, running off in his stripy pyjamas.

'Hey, what about your bed?' shouted the policeman.

'Give it a parking ticket, if you like! I'll be back for it later!'

The townsfolk of Bacteria were treated to another strange sight that morning: the figure they had just seen being towed along in bed was now running through their streets in nothing but his pyjamas!

The bats were wide awake in the Castle clock.

'I say, Dmitri!' said Sviatoslav.

'What is it, my friend?'

'Remember the one about the teacher who's telling little Johnny off for being late for school?'

'Probably – but *do* remind me.'

'Okay. "You should have been here at nine o'clock!" he says, and little Johnny replies – '

'"Why, sir, what happened?"' finished Dmitri.

The bats exploded with mirth.

'I know what reminded you of that joke, Sviatoslav,' giggled Dmitri. 'It's the duck, isn't it? Unless he gets here in ten minutes, the Castle will take us back home without him!'

'Exactly, Dmitri! I suppose he'll have to fly back!'

'The duck – *fly?* He can't do *that!*'

'Why not? He's got the weather for it!'

More uncontrollable bat laughter echoed through the clock and down the empty corridors of the Castle!

Duckula was making good time as he left the town behind and raced along the wide road towards Duckling's. At least he was until he drew level with an old lady struggling along with numerous, packed carrier bags in her hands.

'I say, young man!' she cried in a shaky voice.

'Yes, madam?' puffed Duckula, stopping to talk to her.

'That's a lovely jogging outfit you're wearing! I've never seen a striped one before!'

'You wouldn't believe me if I told you they were my pyjamas!' smiled Duckula. 'Is that all you wanted me for? Only I'm in an awful – '

'Well, not *just* that,' said the old lady hesitantly. 'I wondered if you'd help me carry my bags home. It's not far . . .'

'Oh, but I *can't* – ' began Duckula in desperation.

'I wouldn't ask normally, but they're so heavy!' twittered the lady. 'I've been early morning shopping at the supermarket to get some food in. My son's coming to stay for a few days . . .'

Duckula couldn't possibly refuse. He took the

heaviest bags and trudged along the road with the old lady. His arms ached as precious minutes ticked by. He dearly wanted to put down the bags and run to the Castle.

'It's a lovely sunny day!' chattered the lady. 'Are you down here on holiday?'

'Not exactly. I'm working at Duckling's,' replied Duckula.

'Oh, how lovely! I know Mr Duckling . . . such a *nice* man!'

At length they reached the garden gate of a small, homely cottage.

'Thank you very much,' said the old lady. 'Would you like a cup of tea? Won't take me a minute to put the kettle on!'

'No, thank you very much! I must be off!' answered Duckula, with one eye on the Castle, which was still a few hundred metres away.

Suddenly there came the familiar trembling and aura of pulsating coloured lights around the Castle that signalled its imminent departure. Then, with a dreadful sinking feeling, Duckula saw it disappear!

'I – I'll take you up on that offer of a cup of tea,' he said slowly to the old lady. 'I think I've got all the time in the *world* now . . .'

13
A Miserable Morning

Duckula no longer had any reason to rush back to Duckling's. He strolled along, wondering how he could explain the disappearance of the Castle to Mr Duckling, who was expecting it to be the main attraction of the Gala at ten o'clock – just over an hour away!

He had made up his mind to head straight for the office, but as soon as he entered the gateway to the camp, holidaymakers rushed up to him from every direction and demanded his autograph.

'There he is – it's really *him!*' shouted a small boy.

'Wow! Count Duckula!' yelled a girl. 'And in his *pyjamas* too!'

Duckula had forgotten he was still dressed for bed. He blushed with embarrassment and started running towards his chalet. But that made it worse, for more and more people joined his fans in hot pursuit! It was worse than being a baddie with a posse after you!

He spotted his butler ahead. 'Igor, help me!'

Igor looked round, assessed the situation quickly and began to run wheezily alongside his master. 'I . . . I . . . think, milord, you should make for the safety of your chalet!' he panted.

'That's what I had in mind!' Duckula glanced behind and saw the multitude of cheering fans were gained ground. 'Faster, Igor, faster!'

But outside Duckula's chalet, now in sight, another large group of fans were gathering!

'Better go into *my* chalet!' puffed Igor. 'I'll run on and open the door!'

Duckula was astounded when Igor sprinted ahead of him at an alarming rate. Huh, he thought, why can't he move at that speed when he's at home?

Igor arrived at his chalet and flung open the door. A dreadful sight met his eyes!

'Surprise, surprise!' beamed Mrs Housemartin, standing over the little cooker in the chalet, a frying pan in her hand. 'The way to a man's heart is through his stomach, I always say – so I've cooked you a vegetarian lasagne!'

'How nauseating!' was all Igor could say before he ran out, raced past Duckula's chalet – complete with its crowd of autograph hunters – and opened the door of Nanny's chalet. 'This way, milord!'

Duckula charged into Nanny's chalet; Igor slammed the door shut and locked and bolted it. Frustrated fans banged and shouted for Duckula to come out.

'Gee, if *this* is stardom, I don't want it!' gasped Duckula.

Igor shook his head sadly. 'If your forefathers could see you now, sir, I don't know what they'd say . . .'

'*Four* fathers?! And I thought I only had *one*!' chuckled Duckula, now recovering from his ordeal.

'I fear we shall be holed up in here, as they say, for quite a while, sir. Shall I put the kettle on?'

'Well, as Nanny doesn't appear to be here, I

suppose you'll have to, Igor. Pity *you* don't have a tea-vending sling too!'

When the two Transylvanians had drunk their tea and discussed the catastrophic disappearance of the Castle, Igor settled back in an armchair and Duckula sat on Nanny's bed. He picked up some magazines that she had left on the bedside table and thumbed idly through them. Amongst them was a local newspaper – and on the front cover was a picture of Frankie Fledgling singing in Las Vegas. Duckula examined the picture and practised holding an imaginary microphone in the same slick way as Frankie.

It was then that he read the short text beneath the photograph! He slammed the paper down and let out a long whistle, waking Igor from a doze.

'Is there something the matter, milord?'

'Igor – I've been reading this newspaper article about Frankie Fledgling. He's just finished his American tour . . .'

'How exciting for him!' murmured Igor, putting his head back again and closing his eyes.

'But, Igor, this is the *Bacteria Bugle* – and it describes Frankie as a local boy made good! That means that Nanny was right and he must have started in this very holiday camp!'

'Really, sir?' mumbled Igor, half asleep.

'Yes, really!' insisted Duckula indignantly. 'And it's given me a brilliant idea!'

On the beach, Gala Day was turning out to be a dreadful flop! Mr Duckling was in a terrible plight, trying to make his opening speech as he stood on a raised wooden platform. Around him were despondent Yellowbeaks in charge of various tables packed with free orange drinks, sweets, cakes and buttered scones.

A large crowd of people had turned up but most of them were badly disappointed to find there was no Transylvanian castle to be seen anywhere.

'Where's this castle, then?' jeered one stubborn fellow in a flat cap.

Mr Duckling politely stopped his speech to answer, 'I honestly don't know . . . but if you'll bear with me, I'll do my best to find out!'

This reply was greeted with derisive laughter from the spectators.

'Where's that *fantastic* comedian we've heard about!' yelled a woman.

'Yes, where's Count Duckula? We thought he worked here!' bawled another.

'*I'd* like to know where he is, too!' shouted Mr Duckling over the din made by the unruly crowd. 'Now, if you'd all care to help yourself to some free orangeade and food, you can chat to our friendly Yellowbeaks, who will be delighted to tell you all about Duckling's. And then, in a few minutes, you can all come on a guided tour of the camp!'

'Big deal!' bellowed a ruffian from the back, and everyone hooted with laughter.

'*We want Duck – u – la! We want Duck – u – la!*' chanted a group of teenagers.

Mr Duckling stepped down. Olivia came up to him and passed him a handkerchief to mop his brow. They watched everyone milling around the stalls, grabbing

101

the food and guzzling the orangeade and demanding their free balloons from the disappointed Yellowbeaks.

'Look at *that!*' exclaimed Mr Duckling in a disgusted voice. 'They've come for a free scoff – and now they're all walking off home again without even looking at the camp!'

'This way to Duckling's, ladies and gentlemen!' called Olivia in a vain attempt to interest the few remaining stragglers. 'Come on, now! It's well worth a visit!'

'We'd rather watch the *telly!*' replied an infuriating, smirking young man dressed in shorts and T-shirt and wearing a knotted handkerchief on his head.

It was almost lunchtime before Duckula could escape from Nanny's chalet. He'd found an old coat and put it over his pyjamas, then opened the chalet door to chat to the waiting fans and sign autographs. More and more people had appeared, and it was only the delicious smell of cooking wafting from the dining room that eventually dispersed the crowd and persuaded them to go and eat.

'Boy, I could eat a *horse!*' said Duckula.

'*What* did you say, milord?!' exclaimed Igor, his eyes opening wide.

'Don't get excited, Igor! It was only a figure of speech. But first I must go and apologise to Mr Duckling for letting him down with the Castle. I only hope he doesn't fire me!'

Duckula kept the coat on, pulled up the collar to hide his face and set off for Mr Duckling's office. It took him a while to get there, for whenever he met anyone, he changed direction and did a detour.

And I thought being famous would be *fun*, he mused. It's worse than living in Castle Duckula!

As he reached the office door, a big, rude man in a smart suit came out quickly and almost bowled him over.

'Outa my way, kid!' said the man brusquely. 'Let me get outa this dump!'

Duckula put his tongue out at him – when he was safely out of reach! – and walked into Mr Duckling's office.

Olivia looked up. 'Phew, it's *you*, Count D! For a moment I thought it was E. J. Eagle coming back!'

'So *that* was E. J. Eagle! What's he doing here?'

'I think you'd better ask Mr Duckling that,' she replied. 'You've come to talk to him?'

'Yes.'

'Go straight in. He's free.'

Duckula took a deep breath and marched in with a sunny expression. 'Hi, Mr Duckling!' he said in an unconvincingly chirpy manner.

Mr Duckula was seated at his desk, leaning forward with his head in his hands. He looked up miserably and said, 'Ah Count Duckula . . . I wondered when you'd turn up.'

'I'm sorry about this morning, Mr Duckling. I suppose the Gala went pretty badly . . .'

'The Gala was a *non-event!*'

'What can I say?' said Duckula. 'If I told you what happened, you'd never believe me!'

And Mr Duckling didn't! When Duckula explained

how he'd woken to find himself in a public park, then been delayed by an old lady with heavy shopping and narrowly missed saving the Castle from flying back to Transylvania by itself, Mr Duckling just started laughing at him.

Duckula told him that he'd do anything he could to drum up trade, but Mr Duckling shrugged his shoulders.

'It's no use – only a miracle would save Duckling's now,' he declared. 'E. J. Eagle, the property developer, has been in. You see, I owe a lot of money to this loan company which Mr Eagle has bought out. And because I'm behind with the payments, he's insisting that I pay up everything by noon tomorrow. If I don't, he'll send in the bailiffs and take possession of the place!'

'He can't do *that!*' exclaimed Duckula. 'What about all the people who've booked their holidays here?'

'I'll have to transfer them to the other Duckling's camps. They'll be glad of the extra custom: they're all struggling to keep going,' said Mr Duckling. He banged his fist on the desk in frustration. 'I can't bear to see *this* camp close down! It means so much to me – it's where I started off!'

Just like Frankie Fledgling did, thought Duckula. He rose to his feet and walked round his chair twice, deep in thought.

'I'm sorry, friend, but it looks like the end of your new career as a comedian,' sighed Mr Duckling.

'I don't care about *that*,' said Duckula. He stopped pacing around. 'But I *do* care about your holiday camp – and I promise you here and now that it will *not* close down!'

In the Eagle's Nest!

Jackie Jackdaw's aunt was on the mend, so that evening he was back on-stage at Duckling's. It was just as well, for Duckula had a more pressing engagement – at Readycash Hall, the luxury mansion home of E. J. Eagle!

If you'd been at the end of the long drive leading to the Hall as darkness began to fall, you would have seen a taxi pull up and three figures emerge from it: a smallish duck-like chap in a cloak, a round-shouldered butler and an enormous hen-shaped Nanny! You would have heard the taxi's springs groan with relief as the *last* person got out!

The three Transylvanians crunched along the gravel path which meandered through the meticulously maintained grounds and took them to the imposing front door.

Duckula pressed the ornate brass doorbell button and stepped back, awaiting an answer. He had a determined expression on his face; he would implore E. J. Eagle to leave Mr Duckling and his holiday camp alone. It seemed like a good idea, but he didn't feel *quite* so confident now that he was actually on Eagle's doorstep!

'Ooh!' screeched Nanny, making him and Igor jump in the stillness of the evening. 'Me an' Mr Igor 'ad better go round the back, Duckyboos! There's a little sign 'ere with an arrow, sayin' "Servants and Tradesmen – Rear Door".'

'Stay where you are, please, Nanny,' demanded Duckula. 'I've brought you here for moral support.'

The door was opened by a snooty butler, who seemed to sniff at the visitors.

'Good evening!' said Duckula. 'May we see Mr E. J. Eagle?'

'Have you an appointment?' asked the butler.

'Well, no . . . not exactly.'

'Mr Eagle never sees anyone without an appointment. Goodnight to you.' The butler began to close the door, but Nanny blocked it with her foot.

'"Ere, 'ang on! We've spent good money in a bloomin' taxi comin' 'ere!' she squawked.

'Are you rich? Are you famous?' questioned the butler, eyeing the trio up and down. 'Are you well-connected?'

'I'm a Count!' cried Duckula.

The butler rubbed his chin. 'Very well. Come in and I'll see if Sir is at home.'

'Would you *believe* it!' moaned Nanny, stepping into the huge, wood-panelled hall. 'After all that, 'e don't even know if 'is boss is *in!*'

Igor and Nanny sat on an elegant chaise-longue whilst the butler slipped out of sight through some large double doors. Duckula wandered round the hallway, admiring the expensive-looking paintings hanging on the wall and various other antiques on display.

What a place! he thought. Makes the Castle look like a scrapyard. Hey – the Castle *is* a scrapyard!

106

He tapped the wood panelling to see if it was solid wood or just mahogany-effect. It was solid, right enough, but there was just one panel which sounded rather hollow. Duckula tapped it harder – and then wished he hadn't, for a section of the wall and the floor on which he was standing slid round smoothly and silently, depositing him in another room!

He opened his beak to express alarm, but then he held it shut, for he discovered that he was in the corner of a drawing room – and there, standing over a table littered with aerial photographs of Duckling's, were E. J. Eagle, the butler . . . and Von Goosewing!

'Tell 'em to wait, whoever they are! I'll be with 'em in about half an hour!' snapped Eagle to his butler, who nodded and left the room.

'These photographs are just what I need to map out the initial plans for my new ferry port. You're job is finished now, Goosepimple!' announced Eagle, taking from his jacket pocket a wad of banknotes and handing it to Von Goosewing. 'Here's your dough.'

Von Goosewing took the cash gleefully and counted it quickly. His face dropped. 'I sink there has been some mistake, Mr. E. J. Vee agreed on double ziss amount, ja?'

'That's all you're getting, Gooseberry. Call it deflation, if you like . . . and don't forget that I fell out of your plane twice. A half-baked pilot only gets half pay – ja?'

'Ve'll see about *zat!*' cried Von Goosewing. 'Just vait until TWITS hears about you!'

'And what's TWITS – besides *you!*' guffawed Eagle.

'Two Wings In The Sky – zee international biplane society, which lays down guidelines for. . .'

'Listen, kid!' interrupted Eagle. 'You tell your TWITS whatever you like – they don't scare me *this* much!' He clicked his finger and thumb right under Von Goosewing's nose. 'Nobody scares E. J. Eagle . . . well, except for *this* guy . . .' He picked up a newspaper and pointed out a picture of an extremely tall individual with a big bushy beard, who had been snapped at an airport check-in desk. '. . . Laughing Gerry Ginger from Texas!'

'Oh, really?' said Von Goosewing. 'He sounds quite pleasant!'

'*Pleasant?* Are you kidding, Gooseneck?! He's over seven feet tall with a bright ginger beard . . . and the only time he laughs is when he's up to dirty tricks! He's the scourge of the business world – and he's over here in England, according to the papers . . .'

'Und vhy are you so scared off him?'

'I got the better of him once in a big oil deal – and I wouldn't like to tread on his toes again. He'd ruin me, I know it!'

Bleep, bleep! The conversation was interrupted by the vampireometer on Von Goosewing's wrist. It had detected Duckula's presence!

'Something wrong with your watch again?' snapped Eagle.

'Er – yes, it must be kaput, Mr Eagle!' said Von Goosewing absent-mindedly, switching off the tiny contraption.

Duckula, who had been standing silently in the corner of the room and observing the proceedings, felt that the time had come to leave! He tapped the wooden panelling as hard as he could without making too much noise. Nothing happened at first – but then the secret section of the wall and floor slid round again, transporting him back to the hall.

He found himself behind Nanny's back and he tapped her on the shoulder.

'Ooooh!' she yelled, leaping into the air. 'Oh, Duckyboos, you gave me a proper turn! Where did you come from? I've been lookin' for you!'

'Never mind, Nan,' replied the Count. 'We're off! Come on, Igor!'

'But, milord, you haven't seen Mr Eagle yet,' Igor reminded him.

'I've seen enough!' smiled Duckula mysteriously.

15

Duckula's Master Plan

After breakfast next morning a group of people sat at a table in the dining room, called together for an extraordinary meeting!

Igor and Nanny were there, together with Yellowbeaks Molly and Brian, Olivia, Grandad and Grandma Corncrake with their twin grandsons, and Jackie Jackdaw, who had come from home to be there.

'What's it all about?' asked Olivia.

'Oi be askin' moiself the same question. Oi found this in me dressin' room las' night,' said Jackie Jackdaw, holding up a small, neatly written card, saying:

HELP TO SAVE DUCKLING'S
FROM CLOSING DOWN!

Come to an important meeting
in the Dining Room
tomorrow at 10.30 a.m.

Count Duckula

'I got one too!' declared Molly, waving a similar card.

'Ooh, so did I!' cried Nanny. 'Duckyboos must 'ave been up bright an' early. I found mine pushed under me chalet door!'

It appeared that every one of them had received an invitation from Duckula. But what was he up to?

They soon found out, for at that moment Duckula made his appearance, holding a large cardboard box with both hands.

'Good morning, everyone! Hope I'm not late!' he greeted them, placing the box on the table. 'Thanks for coming.'

He went on to tell them of the terrible fate that Duckling's was about to suffer at the hands of E. J. Eagle. They were all dreadfully upset to hear such bad news.

'But what can we do about it?' asked Olivia.

'We can do a *lot*,' replied Duckula. 'At least we can do our very best! I have a Master Plan! Are you all willing to help?'

'Yes!' cried everyone.

'Help with what?' added Nanny, who wasn't altogether clear about what was going on.

'Oh, Nan, I've no time to explain it all to you. There isn't time to explain anything to *any* of you. Will you all please do exactly as I tell you?'

'Yes!' repeated everyone, boosting Duckula's confidence no end!

'Right, Nanny . . . have you any needle and thread in your sling?'

'Course I 'ave, Duckyboos. Any colour you likes!' Nanny pulled out a handful of brightly coloured bobbins and a pincushion.

'Molly,' he said. 'Did you make that long-distance telephone call?'

'I did,' she smiled. 'And the answer was *yes*!'

111

'Great!' cried Duckula. 'Now, Jackie,' he said, pulling out the old overcoat that he'd used the previous day to disguise himself from his fans. 'I'd like you to search through your props and find another coat about the same shade as this one. And will you bring your make-up kit and false beards and things?'

'Oi will!' Jackie saluted like a soldier and went off to the ballroom.

'How would you twins like to do some acrobatics – like the tumblers in the show?' asked Duckula.

'Not half!' they answered together.

'Right, Tim, I want you to practise walking about with Tom standing on your shoulders. Or you can do it the other way round if you wish!'

The boys were mystified but they did as they were told, and they quickly mastered the required balancing feat.

'That's super – but it must be even better! You've got an hour to perfect it!' said Duckula. He pulled a big roll of paper from the cardboard box and handed it to Grandma and Grandad Corncrake. 'Will you two please catch a bus into Bacteria and ask a printer to make a hundred copies of this poster? Have your lunch out whilst they're being done, then collect them and meet Brian and the other Yellowbeaks in the shopping centre at two o'clock.'

Duckula was like a real business tycoon, dishing out orders to his nodding staff!

'Brian,' he said, 'you and your colleagues will form a team, going round town and putting up posters wherever you can. Okay?'

'Okay,' agreed the puzzled Brian obediently.

Duckula consulted the big clock on the wall of the dining room and rubbed his chin. 'We have a lot to do – and there's not much time!' he murmured. 'Olivia, Igor and Nanny, gather round . . . we have some strategy to discuss.'

'Oo – er!' squawked Nanny. She didn't like the sound of this – *whatever* it meant!

At twelve noon precisely, E. J. Eagle parked his enormous limousine outside the gates of Duckling's.

'She's too big to get through the entrance!' he scoffed, swaggering past the security men. Von Goosewing scuttled along behind him; Eagle had brought him to witness the signing of a legal document, promising that in return he would consider giving him the remaining half of his flying fees!

Harry, at the gate, picked up his phone. 'Action stations, Olivia. He's on the way!'

Eagle entered the office, pushed his way past Olivia and sprawled out in a chair opposite Mr Duckling, who looked very flustered and red in the face. Poor old Von Goosewing stood uneasily between the two of them.

'Good morning . . . I mean afternoon, Mr Eagle,' said Mr Duckling politely.

'Let's cut the small talk,' snapped Eagle. He smiled cruelly. 'Have you got the cheque or not?'

'The *cheque*?'

'Hey, stop playing games, Duckegg. Do you have the money you owe me?' Eagle knew very well that he hadn't!

'Can we talk about it?' asked Mr Duckling.

'We can talk about closing down your holiday camp and building a new ferry port on the site,' grinned Eagle, slapping an important-looking paper scroll on the desk. 'Sign this transfer of ownership – and your worries will be over! My associate, Dr Goosebumps, will witness our signatures!'

Mr Duckling didn't know what to do. There was no way he could pay the debt, yet he hated the idea of pleading with Eagle for mercy.

Fortunately he didn't have to! Because Duckula's Master Plan – or Master Duckula's Plan, as Nanny thought it was called – was put into effect.

Olivia went to the office door and waved a little Union Jack flag – the sort you buy at the seaside to put on your sandcastle – but let's not remind Duckula about *sandcastles*!

Igor, slouching casually against the souvenir shop opposite, saw the signal and, in turn, waved to Nanny, who was waiting round a convenient corner.

'Ooh, Mr Igor's wavin' to me! That's nice of 'im, isn't it, boys?!' she exclaimed, waving back.

'He's giving you the signal, Nanny!' tutted one of the Corncrake twins, who were both waiting with her. 'Hurry up! Give us a hand!'

Nanny helped Tom – or it could have been Tim – to stand on the other's shoulders. Then she draped a huge overcoat round them and fastened up the buttons. Nanny had lengthened the coat supplied by Duckula by sewing on an extra piece of material from a similar garment from Jackie's assortment of theatre props.

The twin on top was wearing some of Jackie Jackdaw's stage make-up, which made him look like a man. And when Nanny reached up and hooked a big, bushy, false ginger beard – also supplied by Jackie – round his ears and dropped a wide-brimmed hat on his head, the illusion was complete: in front of Nanny stood the exact double of Laughing Gerry Ginger from Texas! Even his mother wouldn't have known the difference! But let's leave *her* out of it: this story is complicated enough as it is.

'Off you go, me young fellers,' said Nanny.

The peculiar figure began tottering slowly over towards the Duckling's office, in full view of the window. Every few seconds, the twins made a deep 'Ho, ho, ho!' sound, as Duckula had directed them to do.

'I say, Mr Duckling,' said Olivia, gazing through the office window and pretending to be surprised. 'Here's your old pal Gerry Ginger coming to see you!'

E. J. Eagle almost collapsed with shock. It couldn't be *the* Gerry Ginger, his deadly enemy, could it? He rose shakily to his feet and looked for himself. It was *the* Gerry Ginger – and, yes, he was laughing! That meant trouble for someone!

'What's *he* doing here?' Eagle's voice was high and whining with fear.

Mr Duckling might have answered – *if* he'd had the faintest notion of what was going on!

'Why, Mr Ginger's a very good friend of Mr Duckling. He loves to come and stay at Duckling's at least once a year. It helps him to unwind after all

115

those big business deals he conducts! Isn't that so, Mr Duckling?'

Eagle broke in. 'Let me get outa here! Look, forget the money you owe me, Duckling – you can *have* it! And keep Duckling's just the way it is – a fine place to come for a holiday!'

'That's very kind of you,' said Mr Duckling. 'But I assure you I will pay off every penny of my debt eventually.'

'Just as you like,' said Eagle. 'Only please don't tell Mr Ginger anything about me and those silly plans I had to close Duckling's and build a ferryport!'

'You have my word!' beamed Mr Duckling. How *could* he tell him, when he didn't even know who 'he' was!

Where was Duckula all this time? He was so scared of his Master Plan misfiring that he couldn't bear to watch! So, in order to soothe his nerves, he'd gone for a ride on the dodgems. But he'd forgotten how adoring his fans were; they still hadn't forgotten his marvellous performance two nights before! And when they saw him racing about in a dodgem, they flocked around him, causing a mini traffic jam! The funfair operator had to switch off the power and bring the little cars to a standstill.

Duckula signed endless autographs, but when he saw the crowd growing bigger by the second, he had to escape! He disappeared downwards and tunnelled his way between his fans' legs until he was free!

It took a few seconds for them all to realise that their idol was no longer in their midst, and then one of them caught sight of Duckula sneaking away.

116

They ran after him like pack hounds on a hunt. Duckula ran too and soon found himself near the office with nowhere to hide. When he saw the wobbling ginger giant he'd helped to create, he had a brainwave. Do you know what he did, reader? Yes he lifted the bottom of the coat and crept inside, next to Tom – sorry, Tim!

It was a good job that E. J. Eagle didn't look too closely, or he would have spotted that Laughing Gerry Ginger had four legs. But he didn't, so it doesn't matter!

The figure was now close to Mr Duckling's office window, and Duckula was within the detection range of the pesky vampireometer on Von Goosewing's wrist.

Bleep, bleep! Bleep, bleep! Von Goosewing watched the little finger on the dial spin round and then point towards 'Laughing Gerry Ginger'.

'Sauerkraut und sausages!' he exclaimed. 'Ziss Gerry Ginger fellow ist not just ein bad lot, Mr Eagle – he iss a *wampire* too!'

'My goodness! My neck!' yelled Eagle. 'Well, that does it – I'm *off*!'

And with that, he charged at the office door without even stopping to open it, and smashed right through it – just like Nanny would have done!

E. J. Eagle was gone – and Duckling's was safe!

16
A Surprise Ending!

Duckling's might have been saved from the clutches of E. J. Eagle but there was still much to be done to save it from going into a decline. And Castle Duckula – Mr Duckling's best publicity prospect to date – was no longer around!

Let's take a trip into Bacteria-on-Sea and see how Grandma and Grandad Corncrake were spearheading Phase Two of Duckula's Master Plan!

They had followed Duckula's instructions and caught the number 109 bus into town and found the printer's shop. They gave him the poster that Duckula had drawn up, and he had told them to call back an hour later.

Quite exhausted, they had then repaired to the Greasy Spoon Café where they ordered double egg and chips with bread and butter and tea. Grandma Corncrake had ticked off her husband for making a chip sandwich in public!

At two o'clock they arrived at the shopping centre, where they met up with Brian and his gang. Each Yellowbeak took a handful of posters and spent the afternoon sticking them in shop windows, in the library and anywhere else they could find!

Are you wondering, reader, what the posters said? Well, you *should* be – unless you've guessed already, cleverclogs!

The posters caused quite a stir in Bacteria-on-Sea because they announced a special, once-in-a-lifetime concert that night at Duckling's, starring the legendary, world-famous singer – Frankie Fledgling! Wowee!

The townsfolk were amazed! Those who had trekked to the holiday camp to visit the 'genuine Transylvanian castle' were sceptical, but even they said they must go to the concert if there was a chance of seeing Frankie Fledgling!

Back at the camp, Mr Duckling was learning from Olivia the facts behind Duckula's brainy scheme to rid them of E. J. Eagle. He was still laughing at the ingenuity that had gone into the Master Plan, when he received what he thought was a piece of bad news: because there weren't sufficient funds in the Duckling's bank account to pay him until the following week, guest star Vince Vulture had packed his bags and gone back to London.

'I don't know what we'll do for the show tonight, Olivia,' groaned Mr Duckling miserably. 'If only Count Duckula could sing too . . .'

'Don't you worry about it, Mr Duckling,' said Olivia gently. 'Count Duckula's already planning a surprise for tonight. Just wait till you find out what it is!'

It was early evening when Mr Duckling left his office. His attention was drawn to a commotion at the main entrance, through which a continuous stream of excited, chattering boys, girls, men and women poured into the camp.

119

Mr Duckling walked over to investigate and was shocked to see a huge queue of people on the outside, stretching right back onto the beach. The two security men were collecting money from everyone who entered, and their pockets bulged with the cash.

'Hello there, sir!' cried Harry.

'Good evening, Harry,' replied Mr Duckling. 'What on earth's going on here?'

'You mean you don't *know*?' said Harry.

'No, I've no idea. Why are all these people paying to come into Duckling's?'

'Oh dear, Olivia must have been keeping it as a surprise for you – and now you've found out for yourself! It's Frankie Fledgling – he's appearing here *tonight!*'

'You're *joking!*' exclaimed Mr Duckling, his mouth wide open.

'He's not!' said Olivia's voice from behind Mr Duckling. She linked arms with her boss and pulled him away from the gate. 'Come on, Mr D, before all the best seats are gone!'

The lights dimmed in the packed ballroom and the band began to play. The curtains opened and there in the spotlight stood *Frankie Fledgling*! The audience cheered, clapped, and whistled so much that his singing could hardly be heard at first. He warmed up with a couple of well-known numbers from his repertoire, and then he stopped to chat to everyone.

'Thank you so much. It's a real pleasure to be here – back in my home town of Bacteria-on-Sea,' he began. 'It was in this holiday camp that I began my singing career, and I really owe everything to Mr Duckling for giving me my big chance! So what better way can I say thank you than by appearing here tonight and giving all the proceeds to Count Duckula's super scheme to save the holiday camp from closing down!'

Another spotlight picked out a blushing Duckula, who was sitting in the front row, along with Igor, Nanny, Olivia, Mr Duckling, Jackie Jackdaw, Molly, Brian, all the Yellowbeaks and the Corncrake family! The twins, once so unruly, were now reformed characters and proud to have played their part in helping Duckula.

'And now I'm going to sing "Sunshine, Strawberries and You",' announced Frankie. 'But there's someone I'd like to sing along with me here up here on the stage! Are you there, *Nanny*?'

'Oooooooh!' Nanny let out the longest 'ooh' she had ever squawked. 'I couldn't!'

But she *could* and she *did!* Igor helped her up the steps and Frankie led her to the microphone. And there, holding Nanny in his arms – well, as much of her as he could manage – Frankie sang his best known song!

Nanny was almost crying with delight! For the first time in her life she was speechless. She just kept looking at Frankie and then back at Duckula and Igor. Duckula had a lump in his throat; only now did he realise quite how much those scratchy old records back at the Castle meant to his dear Nanny. Igor was almost crying too!

The concert seemed to go on and on. Frankie sang

song after song until, Duckula thought, his voice would surely give up.

Finally, Frankie *did* sing his final song and the show came to a close with a standing ovation. The rapturous applause and cheering went on for several minutes before the audience began to leave their seats and file out of the ballroom.

The night might have been over for the members of the public – but for those who had taken part in Duckula's Master Plan there was a *party*! All the seats were pushed to the side of the ballroom. Igor and Marcel the waiter, who had now become his firm friend, wheeled in some dinner wagons stacked with drinks and sandwiches. The band stayed behind to provide music, and everyone laughed and talked well into the night!

Nanny tended to monopolise Frankie, but he didn't mind, for he was flattered by her knowledge of his career. She was his number one fan and knew more about him from her fan club magazines than he knew *himself*!

Mr Duckling came over to shake Frankie's hand and thank him for saving Duckling's. 'We've made so much money tonight in takings that we can give the old place a new lease of life – *and* pay off the debt owing to E. J. Eagle. But tell me, Mr Fledgling,' he said. 'How come a big star like you came to help us out?'

'Thanks to Molly, your Yellowbeak,' said Frankie. 'Apparently her friend Duckula asked her to telephone me at my hotel. He'd seen in some newspaper

122

that I had just finished my American tour and was staying in the Golden Beak Hotel in New York.'

'You must have been exhausted!' commented Igor, who had overheard the conversation.

'I was – but there was something else that made me come here,' said Frankie seriously. 'Yesterday I was chatting to my little old mum, who still lives here in Bacteria, and she told me how some kind person who worked at Duckling's helped her to carry her heavy shopping bags home. So how could *I* possibly have refused to help Duckling's . . .?'

Duckula heard this but didn't say a word; he simply stood still, staring into space.

''Appy, Duckyboos?' Nanny brought him back to reality with a hefty nudge.

'*You bet*!' he answered with a grin.

High in the Transylvanian Alps, the bats in the Castle clock had a whale of a time cracking jokes about the sorry plight of Duckula, Igor and Nanny, left stranded in that strange country called England. They fell about in spasms of giggling at the thought of the trio trudging back overland and perhaps even swimming over the sea to get back home. Sviatoslav even suggested sending them a 'Wish You Were Here' postcard!

But the laugh was on the *bats*! They would have been green with envy, had they known that Duckula, Igor and Nanny were living it up free of charge at Duckling's for the next fortnight – with first-class tickets home on the Orient Express from a grateful Mr Duckling.

123

There *were* drawbacks, of course! Duckula had to wear dark sunglasses to disguise himself from his fans; Igor still had to fight off the attentions of Mrs House-martin, who never *did* get him to walk with her on the promenade; and Nanny – well, Nanny just couldn't get used to lounging around with nothing to do! Duckula and Igor had to keep stopping her from attempting to do washing and ironing and brewing tea and making beds; although they did let her continue making cocoa with chocolatey bits on top – as only *she* knew how!

Nothing more was heard about the awful E. J. Eagle, so that just about wraps up the story, doesn't it?

Oh, wait a minute – do you want to know what happened to Dr Von Goosewing? Well, nobody seems to know for sure. It's rumoured that he's still in England somewhere, working in some seaside resort to save up the fare to return home. Seems he never got the rest of his money from Mr Eagle – and his biplane wouldn't make it across the sea; probably not even across Duckling's *swimming pool*!

So, reader, next time you go away, keep a sharp lookout for Goosey. He could be serving you with breakfast . . . putting raspberry on your ice-cream . . . or giving you change on the pier!

If you spot him, don't forget to warn Count Duckula!

Goodnight for now, and thank you for reading this book – *whatever* you are!

Sheep Ahoy!

GRAHAM MARKS AND
CHRISTOPHER MAYNARD

A hilarious collection of extraordinary but absolutely true stories – stranger than fiction – culled from the back pages and people columns of newspapers.

£1.95 □

Mispronts

GRAHAM MARKS AND
CHRISTOPHER MAYNARD

An amusing selection of silly misprints from newspapers and magazines.

£1.95 □

Odd Pets

GRAHAM MARKS AND
CHRISTOPHER MAYNARD

A useful collection of outlandish pets, specially compiled for the lazy pet owner who is not excited by the idea of cleaning out, grooming and feeding. All of the pets to be found in this book are easily obtained, either from the wild, or the human body, and require the minimum of care and maintenance.

£1.95 □

ARMADA

Crazy Curriculum

JONATHAN CLEMENTS

A hilarious alternative look at school education, including study notes on traditional subjects such as history, and not so usual ones such as human behaviour. There are also exam papers and answers, quizzes, timetables and school reports of famous people.

£1.95 ☐

Writing Jokes and Riddles

BILL HOWARD

This is a joke book with a difference – it actually teaches you how to make up a joke! Interspersed with plenty of hilarious examples it also contains a list of key words on which most jokes are based.

£1.95 ☐

Yeuuch!

PETE SAUNDERS

A collection of revolting, horrible and disgusting things you'll wish you'd never discovered that will appeal to those who delight in gruesome detail. All the facts are true and many are highlighted by clever, zany illustrations.

£1.95 ☐

ARMADA

All these books are available at your local bookshop or newsagent, or can be ordered from the publisher. To order direct from the publishers just tick the title you want and fill in the form below:

Name _____

Address _____

_____

Send to: Collins Childrens Cash Sales
　　　　　PO Box 11
　　　　　Falmouth
　　　　　Cornwall
　　　　　TR10 9EN

Please enclose a cheque or postal order or debit my Visa/ Access –

　Credit card no:

　Expiry date:

　Signature:

– to the value of the cover price plus:

UK: 60p for the first book, 25p for the second book, plus 15p per copy for each additional book ordered to a maximum charge of £1.90.

BFPO: 60p for the first book, 25p for the second book plus 15p per copy for the next 7 books, thereafter 9p per book.

Overseas and Eire: £1.25 for the first book, 75p for the second book. Thereafter 28p per book.

ARMADA